MW01127717

To Teddi,
Thanks for your
support! God Bless!

Ted Bagley
10-09-11

The Tragedy of Darkness

The Tragedy of Darkness

Ted Bagley

Copyright © 2011 by Ted Bagley.

Library of Congress Control Number: 2011901950
ISBN: Hardcover   978-1-4568-6541-2
                     Softcover   978-1-4568-6540-5
                     Ebook   978-1-4568-6542-9

All rights reserved. No part of this book may be reproduced or transmitted in any form or by any means, electronic or mechanical, including photocopying, recording, or by any information storage and retrieval system, without permission in writing from the copyright owner.

This is a work of fiction. Names, characters, places and incidents either are the product of the author's imagination or are used fictitiously, and any resemblance to any actual persons, living or dead, events, or locales is entirely coincidental.

This book was printed in the United States of America.

To order additional copies of this book, contact:
Xlibris Corporation
1-888-795-4274
www.Xlibris.com
Orders@Xlibris.com
94194

Contents

"Life isn't tied with a bow but it's still a gift." Regina Brett, age 90

"I refuse to accept the idea that man is mere flotsam and jetsam in the river of life unable to influence the unfolding events which surround him. I refuse to accept the view that mankind is so tragically bound to the starless midnight of racism and war that the bright daybreak of peace and brotherhood can never be a reality.

I refuse to accept the cynical notion that nation after nation must spiral down a militaristic stairway into the hell of thermonuclear destruction. I believe that unarmed truth and unconditional love will have the final word in reality. This is why right . . . temporarily defeated . . . . is stronger than evil triumphant."

—Dr. Martin Luther King Jr.

Acknowledgement

Darkness can be a condition of time or a state of mind. No matter the choice, it represents a period of uncertainty, possible confusion and hopelessness. As a result of the darkness dilemma, I have decided to put on paper my feelings about this dilemma from a common perspective. As kids, most of us were afraid of the dark primarily because of the stories that our parents and grandparents would tell us about the supernatural and other creepy things that only come out in darkness. Naturally we believed it because it came from people close to us who were very credible in our eyes no matter what stories were put before us. In a way it was good because in the early stage of development, it's important that we develop our imagination which would eventually play a major role in our ability to focus on what "could be" versus "what is".

The title of this work is **"The Tragedy of Darkness"**. Now you may say what's so significant about this subject. Being in the dark can be a frightening thing especially if it's not by choice. Things are so much clearer when there is defining light. Try walking into a room where it's pitch dark even if it's in your own home and you will see how difficult it is to navigate around objects that you are familiar with and pass every day while there is light. Most tragedies generally happen under the cover of darkness. If being in the dark is not where you want to be, then what are you doing about it? The real answer is to turn the light on. If only it was that easy.

Mama would say, "Boy, turn on the light in that room, can't you see how dark it is?" Mama was afraid that I would stumble over something and break some of her valuable "whatnots". A "whatnot" was considered any little glass or porcelain figure used to decorate book cases, dressers and nightstands. See if you read my books, you will pick up a lot of terms and information that you didn't know or for those Baby Boomers, hadn't thought about for many years.

What Mama didn't realize at the time was that she was stating a condition that would exist for many generations for men of color. Somewhere in the growing up process, we got off track, lost our way to the light switch and found that we were in pitch dark conditions. Some of these conditions were externally motivated by the media, race relations and history and others were self inflicted. These conditions were confusing, degrading, and just plain frightening.

There is a need to go back, as the old folks use to say, to the old landmarks. There is a need to go back to the way things were years ago when there was respect and dignity for one another, where parents held a high place in the order and where teachers were revered and look up to as the cream of the society's crop. Where kids were required to be in before the sun goes down. Where young people said yes ma'am and yes sir to those considered adults. Where did we go wrong? Somewhere we lost our way to the light switch.

Years ago, we looked forward to a simple cone of ice cream, a butter cookie or a moon pie. A time where kids would get pleasure from squirting each other with the water hose; where sitting down for a game of dominos or checkers was a way to relax; where playing a game of marbles and hop scotch was something to look forward to; where our primary toys were a rick rack, a yo-yo or a bicycle; and where simply making and flying a kite was something to look forward too. Where did we slip on the banana peel? We lost our way to the light switch.

Our young men particularly, could stand an old fashioned butt whipping from Mamas and grandmothers from past generations.

Don't you agree? I don't know about you but those women of experience (you notice that I didn't say old) didn't take any mess. If you were brave enough to talk back to them, it was understood that you would, without a doubt, suffer the consequences. Those consequences could run the gambit from picking a few teeth off the floor from the back hand to the mouth or being banished to the darkest part of the house for the rest of your young life with the only nourishment being bread and water. Maybe it was just simply getting it over by being taken to the wood shed. If you survived, the lesson was learned and though we would do other mischievous things, that particular one would not be repeated until the blisters healed.

Though all of our collective ideas and knowledge will not immediately switch the light on and move us from the darkness into the marvelous light, it will go a long way in publicizing the issue and causing those who choose to come out of the darkness, a method of doing so. The method involves education, knowledge, leadership, honesty, integrity, dependability, spirituality and work ethic and comes with love, sacrifice, patience, involvement and toughness. You can surely take that to the bank.

In the work that follows, I want to introduce you to AJ, a young man who lost his way to the light switch. He had everything going for himself but what follows in this young man's life shows how important it is to come out of the dark into the marvelous light. This is his story.

Chapter I

Things aren't always at it seems . . . .

"The opportunity to practice brotherhood presents itself every time you meet a human being".

Jane Wyman

Chicago, the windy city, a place where the winters are bone chilling cold, the snow has a majestic sense about it as it glistens in the evening sun light. To venture out without gloves or a scarf to cover your face would mean a red nose and blue finger tips. As the days wear on and the traffic and filth mixes creating a muddy and dismal version of it's a dark, dark world. The summers are hot and muggy as a steam room and much too short. Just walking swiftly in the humidity of the summers here creates a sauna like environment. But this is my city and I love it with all of its flaws, scratches and warts on its under-belly.

I grew up on the south side of Chicago, the Washington Park area, better known as the "ghetto". In society's mind, "ghettos" were low-income areas with high incidents of crime and severe poverty but it was much more than that. It housed some of the most talented and misunderstood individuals, who, if given the opportunity, could make significant impact on every aspect of society. Some people are born with silver spoons in their mouths while others have tooth picks. I can still taste the wood from the toothpick so you know I had no silver spoon in my mouth or even in the kitchen drawers.

The slums were even worse than "ghettos" because generally over half of the community lives off welfare and crime is part of the daily smorgasbord. The police tend to stay away from the slums unless they are looking for a reason to use excessive force. Even cab drivers have limits to their lines of demarcation. There are just some places that are not worth risking your life over. There were places like Altegold Gardens in Riverdale where run-down projects and other buildings stand as painful reminders of a hopeless people and Cabrini Green on the North side where drive-by shootings were not the exception but the rule. Why we take hopelessness out on each other I will never understand.

Things were tough for lower middle class families like mine. I define our condition as lower middle class because we were not dirt poor but we couldn't buy things that we wanted and had to settle for the things we needed. We were closer to the "have-nots" versus the "haves", if you know what I mean. There were few if any white slums and even the Hispanic neighborhoods were mostly working class folks with decent jobs. All of the worst parts of Chicago were over 95% African American and Latino. In places like Englewood, Fuller Park, Woodlawn, North Lawndale, Grand Boulevard and Riverdale, it seemed that over half the population in these areas lived off welfare or other government assistance program. It was not because they wanted too but that's the hand they were dealt.

Some self—proclaimed economic brain-e-acts, who didn't know crap about how we survived from check to check, would say that we should "pull ourselves up by our own boot straps" but some of these particular boots were strapless, if you get my drift. It's easy to generalize and say that folks should be able to get themselves out of poverty but so many became a victim of their environment. Not much required, not much desired.

Gang banging was a way of life in and around the city that I called home. If you lived in the 79th street area, it was controlled by the "9", the low end around 53rd and Daman were controlled by the M.O.E'.S and the Hooks and the Westside was dominated by the Vice Lords. No, I was not one of those who sought the gang bang life for security, though it crossed my mind more than a time or two. Anyone who couldn't see that gangs were a losing proposition must have been stuck on stupid. Every week, the meat wagon was hauling away another casualty of the street war that became a way of life in my "ghetto".

I have seen them as young as elementary school sucking the earth before they had a chance to learn their multiplication tables. The mothers who grieved for them were, in more cases than not, still a child themselves. I was determined that my little sister would not end up that way. Some of the caskets were no bigger than an over sized cooler. It was not unusual to find Glock 22c, GSG 5, 357's or 45's tucked in book bags and lockers in elementary and middle schools, when many of these kids should have been enjoying just being a kid and in school learning History, English, and Math, etc., Instead, they were learning how to survive on the mean streets of Chi Town. Guns and drugs were as easy to get as stealing an orange from the local street vendors. Just walking down the side streets and allies in "ghetto hell," the pushers would be selling their products ranging from designer clothes to designer drugs and sophisticated automatic weapons.

During the warmer weather, if you wanted to check out the honeys, you would clean up your ride, put a good spit shine on the 22's and head for Rainbow Beach, Hood Beach, Private Beach or the Point. Man some of these sisters had no right to be so fine. String bikinis ought to be outlawed because the eyes are not designed to take the kind of punishment dished out by some of these Chicago honeys. Some women should have to audition for permission to wear some of the outfits that are on display at the beach fashion show. They truly give rise to the meaning of fun in the sun.

When a woman starts approaching 175 pounds, it behooves her to cover that big ass with a table cloth or something. Man, some of those big girls have no shame. I bet it takes them half a day to find that string once it is consumed by their hippo like rear ends. Man, a brother had to be on his P's and Q's with these fine hamma's or they would hen peck a brother into thinking he is all of that when actually they were spinning that web of deceit to wipe a brother out.

The drug running through the veins of those living in the many ghettoes of Chicago is called poverty. The half way houses were filled with people who were bankers, lawyers, business owners and professors at some time in their lives but a single miss calculation, a bad decision, or a missed calibrated investment had sent them into a spiral of misfortune and depression. You can bet that drugs were somewhere in the mix. When people lose hope, it becomes easy to get lost in the temporary relief of dope. What they fail to realize is that on the other side of that false high is an even greater and deeper low. At the end of each needle was an arm attached to a problem. Hope is an effective weapon against poverty because it gives you the strength to continually "get up" and shake off the dirt from the fall.

Like many other families, my folks were struggling day to day to just make ends meet. They made some decent money but it wasn't mine. My Mama would slide me a 20 spot here and there but I didn't feel very good about it. I wanted to be in a position to take care of her some day. My Pops didn't control the money in our house, so it was useless to ask him for anything. The dude worked his ass off and brought every cent home to moms. I have to give them their due because they would always have food on the table and clothes on our backs, which was more than many who suffered through this war of poverty. People were freaking out over making sixty and seventy thousand big ones which I didn't understand because my mind was stretched out on the Oprah and Tiger Woods type cash.

Selling drugs was the means to an end for a lot of folks who had a death wish but I couldn't cross that line, big money or not. I saw what drugs did to those close to me and around me and I was determined not to be controlled by anything or anybody but me. Life was hard enough without waking up every day having to dig out from not only your condition but also your habits. After seeing my uncle Richie go from being one of the sharpest, best dressed analyst on Wall Street to a half way house, had convinced me that taking the high road made more sense. This dude, at one time, drove around in a steel grey Porsche, wore the finest of Faregamo shoes especially designed and cut for him in New York City. Uncle Richie had class and was always seen with some of the finest arm candy in Chicago. They were not just pretty faces looking for a way out of a dismal situation, but instead from MIT, Harvard, Yale, Brown and other Ivy League rich institutions. Now, just a shell of a man, Uncle Richie spends his days staring out of an open window. A bad investment, loans to family and the high life, had broken this icon of a man. Life had taken his will. When hope is gone, drugs seem to temporarily ease the pain.

Tracks littered the arms of the young and old, the clean and the unclean, white and black, rich and poor. Drugs became a means to an end for many who gave up hope for dope. The real money was not made by those who sold the drugs but by those outside who were capitalizing on the hopelessness and mental weakness of the least, the last and the lost. The real losers were a generation of young brothers who became pawns and runners for the scum bags who lured them with money and hope but gave them Crack.

Drugs did not originate in slums of Chicago but it definitely thrived there as it did in many low income parts of many neighborhoods in the cities. You name it . . . it was available on the street. Anyone could get guns, marijuana, cocaine, uppers, downers, and the universal drug of choice . . . alcohol. The cops knew that this poison and hopelessness was everywhere and chose to simply look the other way. Some even capitalized on the flow of dirty money into our neighborhoods by making their late night visits with their hands out for kickbacks. The drug money greased the pockets of some of the most powerful people in Chicago. In the areas most of us considered to be "across the tracks," the local officials were content to let us kill, steal, rob and shoot up as long as we paid our block fees and kept away from their neighborhoods.

## Chapter II

I am who I am . . . .

Excuse me . . . . I am so caught up in my personal plight and the sad state of affairs around me that I totally forgot to introduce myself. My name is AJ and I want you to remember that. The AJ stands for August James. Why my parents would name me after one of the months of the year, I do . . . not . . . know. Maybe it was because the month of August is named for the Roman Emperor Augustus. Augustus was a bad dude, so that's got to be the reason. If it's not, that's my story and I am sticking to it. I was the down side of two children born to my parents. The other was a down-right fox of a sister named Chantal. She had honey brown hair that flowed like a cool quiet stream on a summer day. Her eyes were as brown as her hair and she was gifted with the brains that I could only wish for. There were a lot of years between us but she was my heart and soul.

Man, I dreaded the day that some dude was going to come to our front door trying to push up on her because if he did, he was going to have me to deal with and that's a fact. My conscious was bothering me because I knew how I was and I knew these hard legs from all over town would be licking their chops to get at Chantal. I was the focus of many a dude who knew I had my eyes on their sisters just as I feared would happen to Chantal now. Just thinking about her brings a smile to my face.

I was the child that every parent wanted but soon wanted to forget. My folks tried their best to bring me up right and place me in the right schools but I had rejected their attempt to make me one of the preppy "wootzies" that walk around with their sweaters around their neck, a Timex watch, an array of Dockers in their closets and at least two pairs of penny loafers stuck under their beds. I was determined to do it my way. I stopped short of having my pants hanging half off my butt, but all of the other teenage traits were definitely in my portfolio. Chugging beer, smoking a joint, staying out all night and putting a notch in my belt for every pair of legs that was caught on my joy stick, was my legacy. All of us that grew up in the stiffening grip of poverty did our share of shop lifting, stealing from the local fruit stands and tossing a brick through a neighbor's window but we controlled our streets. Poverty did not remove the respect that people had for the older members of the community. Even Ned the wine-o said yes sir and yes ma'am to the Patriarchs and Matriarchs on the block.

My folks were hardworking people but the pressures of making ends meet were too much and they eventually tried to solve their problems at the bottom of a Crown Royal bottle. As bad as that might seem, they were not the hard—core element that consumed cough syrup or took the uppers or downers or had tracks in their arms just to ease the pain of hopelessness. They had tried and tried to do it the old American way but that same American way kept slapping them in the behind. Every time they took a step forward there were two steps backwards waiting to smack a hickey on their asses. After Uncle Sam got his piece and the bills were paid, there was little left to do other things like get a better TV or have more than one pair of sneaks under my bed. We always had food in the cabinet though Moms would burn water. It was dangerous having moms anywhere near a stove. My Pops was an easy going passive type who had to get pissed off before he would come close to raising his voice. That was fine with me because I didn't want to hear that lip flapping anyway. My Moms had finished her degree in Marketing from the University of Chicago, Midway, while Pops spent 4 years at Indiana University where he received a Bachelor's Degree in Business Administration. What had happen to my parents had caused me to place limited value on what an education could do for me. Life gets you to a point where you start to doubt whether things will ever get better and once that happens, hell . . . . its got you. Life is what you make it, not what it makes you. It was a lesson that came hard to me.

After years of watching my folks fall down, get up and fall down again, they resorted to running from their problems and throwing down liquor like it was water. I tried the wine and liquor scene myself but it didn't fit my social appetite and quite honestly, a waist of good grapes. Riding the white horse (cocaine) was not my "thang" either but I have to admit, I did dabbled in the hallucinating weed from time to time. It gave me a sense of calm that usually eludes me as I sought my daily dose of sanity in the streets of ghetto hell.

This part of Chicago that time seems to have forgotten, may have been where I started but it is not where I plan to finish and you can take that to the bank cause it's money. The Windy City had become a curse for richly talented as well as naive opportunist like me. The streets had claimed many a good man from living beyond their means trying to satisfy women who preyed on the weak minded and those they thought to have deep pockets. These cougars and Bear-rillas would drain them dry and left them cold and angry at the world for allowing themselves to be suckered like a mouse in a trap. When they finally did come to their senses, their cars and homes were repossessed and their bank accounts were so low that there was not a need to even get a monthly statement. Now that's low. Many had only enough money left in their accounts to keep it open.

After finishing high school, I was offered scholarships both academically and athletically at UCLA and Northwestern. I was not as naturally smart as Chantal but what I lacked in brain overdrive I made up in hard line bull shit and street savvy. I was primarily bored throughout my high school experience because things came pretty easy to me and I was able to charm my way through the early grades. I was semi-smart but lazy, creative but lacked motivation. Grades were not that hard to come by but they were less important to me than those stone cold Michael Jordan moves on the "B—ball" court.

Call it what you want but "B-ball" was money and plenty of it and I was about getting my share. I wanted to one day be able to drop a cool hundred in old homeless Jake's pencil cup on the corner of third and Main. Right now and based on the cobwebs in my pockets, I need to be nuzzling up to old Jake and holding a cup or something myself. I didn't have a pot to piss in or a window to throw it out of. They say that the almighty dollar is the root of all evil but let me have some evil. Going to school, macking girls, having your own crib, paying bills and keeping petro in the ride require some of that evil and I was all about getting my share no matter the consequences.

I finished high school with a respectable grade point average and my basketball skills were enough to get me in to Northwestern. I knew then that I was wasting my time but I was tired of hearing Mom's mouth because of her and Pop's having finished college. There were many days that our conversations got down right combative. I remember this one day that I walked in the house expecting a little peace and quiet when Moms just couldn't resist pulling my chain and the sparks started to fly. "AJ, have you been down to school to check on those transcripts?"

"No Moms but I will when I get time so quit trippin". "AJ, I swear you are one lazy soul. How you figure to get a good job if you don't get into college. And how can you get in college if you don't get that registration finished?" "Moms you are talking smack cause both you and Pops finished and look what it's gotten you?"

The next thing I knew I was picking myself up off the floor. "Boy I brought you into this world and I will take you out if you think you can stand here and disrespect me like that. YOUR FATHER AND I MAY NOT HAVE MUCH BUT WE WORK HARD TO MAKE ENDS MEET AROUND HERE. YOU GOT FOOD ON THE TABLE, THE LIGHTS, ARE ON AND YOU HAVE CLOTHES ON YOUR TRIFFLING BEHIND AND EVEN A LITTLE SPENDING CHANGE . . . . AND WE HAVE TO SIT HERE AND LISTEN TO YOUR CRAP!!!!!. WHERE DID IT ALL COME FROM ? CERTAINLY NOT FROM THE SWEAT OFF YOUR LAZY BEHIND."

Moms truly loved me and I knew it and it was the first time I had ever seen her lose it like that. Man I struck a nerve that I never want to ever strike again. Pops just stood there shaking his head. "Boy, you know you deserved that and as long as you are in this house, you will respect your mother and me. If you feel like you can't do that then you know what you gotta do."

Pops was a man of few words but when he did speak you knew he was serious. Man I wanted to walk out right then and never come back but common sense told me that they were right and it would still be a while before my walking away would be permanent. I knew that I had to go to school or be doomed to this environment for the duration and that wasn't even an option.

That verbal scolding didn't feel good but it hit home with me and it would be the last time I put myself or my parents through that. I was still sitting on the floor with my arms around my knees still smarting from the Hurricane Katrina like tongue lashing. I looked up into their faces and felt like hell because they were right. I was being a son-of-a-B and everyone knew it. As Moms and Pops turned to walk away, I said in a trembling voice, "Mom, ... I am so sorry for what I said and I truly didn't mean it. I was just being stupid and I am so sorry. If you guys want me to leave, I will?" They turned around and just stared at me but didn't say a word. I knew they didn't want me to leave but I didn't know what else to say.

That evening, I casually made it down to the registration office to finish my papers and get a list of my classes for the upcoming school term. Even though UCLA was very attractive and would have made it possible for me to play in a premier basketball program, Chicago was home and all of my home boys and particularly the ladies could not survive without old AJ being on the scene.

I had to do the school thing, one to satisfy my folks and the other to get the mad money that I needed. Most of my road dogs were hanging on the corners, smoking weed, telling lies and watching big ass women walk by. Most of them had no ambition and college was out of the question though many of them had more smarts than I could ever be capable of, I grudgingly admit. Many of these dudes could talk Wall Street with the best of them and kept current on what was going on politically but felt that a formal education was not in their DNA.

The day had come for final registration and I had decided to ask Moms to go with me, hoping that she would have sobered up from the scolding high I had placed her on. I walked to her bedroom door and asked, "Moms would you mind going with me to get the final registration done." She had me on the silent treatment for a few days so I didn't know what to expect. She turned and looked me squarely in the eyes as only a mother can do and I couldn't help but drop my head. "AJ, yes I will go with you but I must be back before 4:00 pm, I have to get down to the salon because I have two good customers that I have to squeeze in today." "OK, most stuff is done; I just have to go to the bursar's office to pay my tuition." It was necessary to have her go with me because the initial jack had to be put down on my courses and I had nothing in my pockets but little balls of paper from the washing machine. You know how the paper in your pants role into lint balls in your pockets when the pants go through the washing machine. Moms and I headed to the car port to get into my ride. As I started to get in on the driver's side, I noticed that Moms was still standing on the passenger side with her arms folded looking at me. "What", I said. "AJ, GET YOU GOOD FOR NOTHING BUTT OUT OF THAT CAR AND COME AND OPEN MY DOOR. I AM GOING TO TEACH YOU SOME MANNERS IF IT KILLS ME." "My bad Moms, you know you raised a gentleman, all the ladies tell me that." "If they call you a gentleman, then I question their "Lady" title.

It was now approaching noon time and I wanted to get this over with. The registration lines were long and I wasn't one with a lot of patience. As I stood in line, waiting my turn to get to the registration window, I couldn't help wondering if the honeys are as cute as some that I had seen. If so, then this could be a very productive and rewarding experience. Just as I leaned against the wall to take a little of the load off, this perfect "10" walked by and went straight into the office. I couldn't help following the motion of that ocean cause she had curves in places that other girls didn't have places.

"AJ, keep your mind on what you are here for and off that girl's butt." "Mom, please chill . . . you know Pops was peeping on your attributes too when you were in college and I have to admit, I don't blame him a bit." "Boy you better hush, I'm your mother and my attributes are none of your concern. Is that all you men think about?" "No, not all, but most", I said with a smile. "Ain't nothing like getting that honey from the bee hive and hope not to get stung." "AJ, you are a heathen and stop saying ain't. It's like you don't have any home training. I hate to say it but standing in this line is most likely a waste of time but you are going to school boy", as she reached up and gave me a playful slap on the back of my head. "You have no respect saying that stuff in front of me", she said. I reached and grabbed her and gave her a hug which brought out the most beautiful smile. I knew how to get to Moms. She loves me and that was no question and I appreciated it though I didn't know how to show it most of the time.

Just as quickly as she had appeared, the honey that glided by us a few minutes before had made a return trip. "Mama, watch this.

Let me show you how bad your son is. Watch, she will walk by then stop and give me that sexy look and play the hard card, then give me those digits. If she does that, I got her, now watch the champ go to work." "Hey there girl, my name is AJ, what's yours?" She walked a few steps past us, stopped and turned around and said, "Hay is for horses and I know you can come better than that." It's Tanya and not Girl." "I stand corrected Miss Tanya. Tanya, meet my mother Rachael James." "Please to meet you Mrs. James. I know you taught him better than that." As she turned to leave, "Mrs. James, it was indeed a pleasure meeting you in spite of your lame offspring. You are a classy lady, I can tell. I hope some of it will eventually rub off if you know what I mean." They gave each other a high five and Tanya was off with an extra wing of the hips and a sassy smile as she slid away . . . . with a final, "goodbye to you too Boy." "I got your boy right . . . . ", before I could finish, Moms popped me again. "AJ, THAT'S WHAT I AM TALKING ABOUT, that mouth of yours need some Clorox." "But Moms, I can't let her front on a brother like that and you giving her a high five and all."

Moms covered her mouth to keep from laughing out loud. Then without even thinking about it said, "You go girl." I couldn't believe that I had been played in front of my moms. "Moms, chill with that." "AJ, what champ . . . you must have meant chump. Any self—respecting woman wouldn't respond to that weak line you just laid on Tanya", said Rachael. "She seemed to be a nice and respectful girl and it seems you can learn a thing or two from her. Actually AJ, that's an example of you thinking with the wrong head my young Nubian offspring. Now put your loins back in your pants and get up to that window and register." To say the least, I was embarrassed because that had always worked until now. Tanya must know that there will be a pay day in the offering. I will hunt her ass down and prove to her that I am nobody's whipping post. Nobody diss old AJ without getting something in return.

Moms wanted to escort me to school on the first day but there was no way I was having that. That's the ultimate embarrassment having your moms show up like she did when you were in elementary school. My first day on campus was uneventful. It consisted of brief visits to each class on the schedule, a visit to the book store and on to the cafeteria. As I strolled into Smith Hall where the cafeteria was located, I looked around as if I was a tourist in New York City. There were students everywhere, none of which were familiar to me. These faces were light years away from Pookie, Cat Daddy and Maurice, my closest acquaintances. I wasn't feeling like conversation so I got a sandwich and a soda and went to the farthest end of the cafeteria where there were many empty tables.

It was fun people watching and I have to admit that there were some well structured women walking around. It was like the United Nation, women of every color and size. Just as I stood to get rid of my trash, a voice came from behind me. "Hey Boy, I mean AJ . . . how are you?" As I turned to return the sentiment, it was Tanya grinning and skinning because she had fronted a brother. I just stood staring at her and she knew why. With a big smile, she said "AJ, no hard feelings about the other day, right?" "Wrong, my sarcastic and not so funny sister, you don't get off that easy. You made a brother look bad in front his Moms and I won't forget that, you can believe that." "AJ, you brought that on yourself and you know it."

Man this girl had an edge about her that pissed me off but was drawing me to her at the same time. "The way you approached me . . . in front of your mother . . . . was "bush" and you know it. No woman wants to be addressed as hay girl!" I will be in the cafeteria around this time every day so if you want to have lunch and talk, I am available."

I was standing there virtually in shock. No woman has ever been so aggressive toward me and I didn't quite know how to deal with it. "That's cool Tanya, take care." I left her standing and watching my back as I walked away. A few days later, I saw Tanya walking hand in hand with an East Indian guy. I didn't even know this lady but I was feeling cheated on. I followed them for a few minutes long enough to see him give her a kiss as they went separate ways. I hurried to catch her before she went to class. "Tanya, ... hay hey Tanya, ... wait up." "Oh, hi boy", said Tanya with a mischievous grin . . . "How are things with you? How are your classes going?" "Now you got to cut that 'boy' shit Tanya, enough is enough. As to your question, the classes are fine, what about yours?" "Everything is cool with me also. So you're talking to me again", she said with a smile. "Yes, I'm cool as long as you cut out that "boy" shit. I couldn't help but notice the guy you were walking with, is that your" . . . , before I could get it out, Tanya said, "Oh, that was Rahem, my husband." "Tanya, you're married?" "Yes I am, and happily. Is that a surprise?" "I have to admit that it is because I thought . . . . "You thought what, that I would fall for that weak line of yours and that I was available? AJ, first of all, you are not my type and secondly Rahem and I have a daughter. We are both here to finish our Doctorial programs, him in medicine and me in Finance. Guys like you are simply pretty faces and often empty on the inside. Not trying to hurt your feelings but I call them like I see them. You seem to be a nice guy AJ, but I can already tell that you lack focus. We can be friends but that has to include Rahem. I have to go, must meet a friend at the library."

I had been fried, dyed and laid to the side, and there was nothing I could do about it. I had indeed met my match. In fact she was more than a match for me and even if she had been single, I am afraid that she wouldn't have found her way into my little black book. What I did realize was that she was the standard that eventually I aspired to have as a companion. I was impressed as well as disappointed. What continues to stick in my craw is her saying that I wasn't her type. I agree with her about the pretty face thing but *what type am I?* "

I, once again, turned my attention to the basketball court. Married or not, sooner or later, Tanya will have to tell me what she meant about not being her type. I guess she like guys with all brain and no game. But it also seemed that the old game of mine needed a bit of polishing.

Chapter III

The Beginning of basketball season

The streets of Chicago produced dudes who could compete with the best minds on the planet, play B'ball at the Michael Jordan level and totally crush a dude on the football field. Instead, most of them ended up like O.J. Simpson with numbers on the front of their uniforms instead of the back. If the military didn't get them, the drugs usually would.

Ball'ing came natural to many of us in the hood. Being the starting forward on the varsity basketball team at Northwestern, hoops were easy to me as was attracting the attention of the cream of the crop of fine women on campus and the pro scouts that would show up every now and then. At 6'2" and averaging a respectable 28 points, 10 rebounds and 8 steals per game, I was a pretty hot ticket on the pro scout's notebook from the very beginning. Coach kept telling me to put some meat on my narrow ass because the big forwards would eat me alive. I like my skinny ass because it allowed me to fit in tight spots if you know what I mean.

My Pops always told us that everyone was just one bad situation away from the soup line. The older I got, the more I understood what he meant. Many of the halfway houses were filled with doctors, lawyers and business men who had the world on a string but through sheer bad luck or a misplaced or ill advised decision, had found themselves living in hopelessness and despair.

The coach at Northwestern, "Big House" Boyd, took a special interest in me primarily because of my skills but I must have taken a few years off of his life because of my lack of a solid work ethic. He was called "Big House" because the arena at Northwestern was huge and he was an imposing figure. He stood 6 feet 5 inches tall with his plaid bow tie, suspenders, and a cigar that was never lit and hung from a mouth that seemed to stretch from one ear to another. He had a voice that pierced the heavy air of the gym like a hot knife through butter. I have yet to see anyone push up against "Big House." They knew better. The dude had arms like tree trunks and just had to look at a brother and you knew that you were in his house and to come right or suffer the consequences.

When you think of someone called "Big House", you automatically think of a large imposing black dude, but this "Big House" was as white as the sheets on my bed and could knock a hole in a brick wall. He was responsible for more dudes going to the NBA than any other college coach except John Wooden at UCLA. "Big House" thought that with enough coaching and counseling, he could make me out of a model citizen. What he didn't know was that I could take the game or leave it. I wanted the glory of what the game could do for me financially but those hard two hour practices, and sweating until I was exhausted from the suicide sprints and jumping jacks wasn't the way I wanted to spend my evenings. I was constantly late for practices, showed little interest in the film sessions prior to games and my arrogance even surprised me at times.

I was out of shape and I knew it, the coach knew it and my team mates knew it. I was either going to make this a serious attempt at basketball or call it quits. I was talented and gifted but severely unfocused and naive to the politics of success and I enjoyed smoking a little gitty-up weed at times. It cleared old AJ's head and made me think clearly. I should have been thrown off the team a long time ago but Coach Boyd had this soft spot for me which I never appreciated. He would say, "AJ, you are a waste of two legs and balls. I am wasting my time thinking that you will ever amount to anything. I don't know why I waste my time." Maybe he was right. But like my parents, he wanted something for me that I didn't seem to want for myself.

In our first scrimmage game with the University of Wisconsin, I stunk up the place with poor shooting and even worst defense. It was the first time that I had heard boo's in my career and it didn't feel good. I had a reputation to uphold and if I couldn't play any better than this in the next game, I may as well pack it in and you know old AJ ain't no quitter so I knew what I had to do. The next practice, I was there before the rest taking free throws and doing wind sprints. When Coach got there I had already worked up a big sweat and was eager to start the shoot around.

When the coach approached me with this look of disbelief in his big bloodshot eyes, all I could say was, "what." "AJ, are you ok, what's going on? You never show up on time and not warmed up. Don't get me wrong, I have been waiting on this for a long time so what gives?" "Coach, can you do me a favor and allow me to speak to the team before we start?" "All right AJ, what's the deal here?" "Coach, just trust me this one time." "All right AJ, but this had better be good."

I grabbed a basketball to put in my hand because it tends to put me at ease. I looked around the group of guys and made eye contact with each of them before starting. "Listen guys, I'm not good at this but I want to sincerely apologize to all of you for not giving it my best against Wisconsin. I let you down, the coach down, and above all, I let myself down and I promise never to allow that to happen again. I appreciate the coach for putting up with me and my attitude over the last few months. The coach should have kicked me off the team but for whatever his reason, he didn't. He gave me the chance that I needed to see if I could help the team. If you guys don't want me around, I understand, but I really do love playing on this team with you guys and if you give me another chance, I won't let you down."

Bo Dickey, an All American point guard spoke up, "AJ as far as I am concerned, you don't deserve another chance. We have put up with your mess since the beginning of the season because you are a good player but no more. This little display of seriousness is a show and I don't believe one bit of it." There are a lot of good players on this team that care about winning and are not as selfish as you are." From that point, I heard a lot of "that's right" and "yea" coming from the peanut gallery, which told me that I was not going to be supported any more by these guys. Just as I turned to walk away, I heard Coach say, "I know I am not hearing what I think I heard. Bo, of all people you should be willing to give someone a second chance after I bailed your tail out of being suspended for low grades didn't we? With a bowed head, Bo said "yes coach." The coach went on, "Some of you others like Sam and Ron . . . didn't you get a second chance when you were accused of breaking into the women's dorm. Even though no harm was done, you both faced suspension until my coaches got involved and pleaded with the Chancellor to give your butts another shot. I am very disappointed in all of you including you AJ. I have favored you during times when I should have kicked your butt off the team. I saw something in you that even you didn't see in yourself. There is no "I" in team and from this point forward, I will be the only one to use "I" in a sentence . . . . do all of you understand? AJ is still our team member until I say differently so if some of you have a problem with that, then you have the right to walk right now." The gym fell silent and no one dared move an inch. The silence lasted, it seemed, 10 minutes when it actually was only a few seconds before coach said, "all right then, let's get to work and prepare to kick some Ohio butt next week."

Believe me, it was the best thing that could have happened to me. Basketball was important to me and it had begun to change my attitude about my classes as well. I was back on the right track. We all need a little kick in the tail at some point. For some unknown reason, I was being given a second chance and I wasn't about to throw it away. In the next game with Ohio State University, I was my old self again. Though I didn't try to score much in that game, I played a smothering defense, had 9 steals and 14 rebounds. I wanted to show the team that I was a complete player and not just a scorer. The next 3 games, with my team again solidly behind me, I averaged a respectable 18 points 8 rebounds and 6 steals per game. Coach had such a big grin on his face that several times he dropped that huge cigar from his lips which had never happened before. I was once again back on track but for how long.

After the game as I walked toward the library a voice called out to me, "AJ . . . . AJ . . . . wait up, I want you to meet Rahem, my husband." Quite honestly, I had no desire to meet this guy. "Oh, hi Tanya." "Rahem, this is AJ . . . AJ, meet Rahem." "Hi Rahem, good to meet you." "Rahem, AJ was trying to hit on a sister but I have my arm candy right here." She reached up and gave him a very tender kiss on the cheek. "Rahem, Tanya is trippin, you have a lovely wife but I was not hitting on her." "AJ, it's good to finally meet you. Tanya told me about you and don't feel bad Bro, all the guys hit on my Tanya. She is indeed a piece of heavens pie." "Look babe, I have to run so nice meeting you AJ, and I will see you at home my love."

I stood watching Rahem disappear between the buildings. I turned to Tanya, "Why did you tell him that I was hitting on you?" "Why not AJ, I have nothing to hide. You know you were hitting on me, that's why you were so shocked when you saw me with Rahem. Rahem and I are comfortable with each other and he is not the jealous type. He knows that I will be home just like he said. Are you telling me that if I wasn't married AJ, that you wouldn't have gone after all of this", as she rubbed her hands from her waist down her hips? "Tanya, you are nice but old AJ can do better, my conceited sister." "AJ, you are a liar and the truth ain't in you." Tanya started to close the space between us. "If what you say is true, then what's that bulge in your pants", she said as she turned to leave. I was like a kid who had just been caught with his hand in the cookie jar. All I could do was stand there with my hands covering my rock hard member. She had done it again. This woman had my number and she knew it. I had never met anyone who had as much charisma and confidence as Tanya and I could tell that she was off limits to me and everyone else . . . except Rahem.

I had to stay away from this man killer or lose my player card. Not only was she fine as hair on a flea's ass but the girl had the academic thing down pat too. I found out later that she and Rahem lived in a large estate near the Gold Coast, one of the wealthiest neighborhoods in Chicago. She was right; I wouldn't know what to do if I did have a woman like her. Women like Tanya make the normal players look like amateurs.

From that point on, I made it a point to not hang around the areas where Tanya would be seen. She had my nose so open that you could drive a Mack truck through it. I had decided to focus on my studies which shocked even me. Focusing was difficult enough with the sights on campus but I was determined not to let Moms down. Just as things were starting to click in the class room, my old habits started to surface again.

Chapter IV

Reba and Faye

Other than that occasional weed, the one thing, on the Northwestern campus that did peak my attention was a perfect ten named Reba who had hips that could sink ships. She was tall, quiet and the envy of every girl on campus because of her academic focus, high moral standards and that killer body that every guy on the yard wanted but was afraid to try for fear of failure. She must have been the product of a mixed marriage because she had long black wavy hair, vanilla ice complexion and blue eyes that were pleasingly angelic. Just one long stare from that perfect ten could make a brother lose his rocks right there on the spot.

Though Reba was capable of crossing over at any time because of her looks, it was obvious that she was black through and through. Her walk, her talk and her attitude let you know that without a doubt she was definitely a sister beyond any stretch of the imagination. She did not hang out with the posse after class because she was too busy working on the school's newspaper and spending her life in the library. Reba was unlike the other girls because she covered up all of her goodies. She wore long flowing skirts and blouses that came to the neck. The girl showed no cleavage at all but you could tell she had a brick house under that Mormon looking outfit that she usually wore. Every now and then she would wear something relative short to her standards and that's when you knew that she had a booger bear under there. I don't know if it was her exotic looks with her long flowing black hair or her mysterious nature that drove me crazy but whichever it was, it had put a love-hook in old AJ.

I was once again the hottest thing on the yard because of my basketball skills and Reba still didn't care if I existed or not. The jocks usually had their way with the women on campus but getting this one would be tougher than breaking into Ft. Knox. I wanted no parts of being the hunter because I was already at the top of that game. I wanted to be the hunted and specifically hunted by the only woman that made me forget the likes of Beyonce' and Janet Jackson. This girl was breaking my cool and I didn't like it at all.

Many of these flake heads on the yard thought that Reba was left handed because they never saw her with any guys on campus. If that was true, then what a waste of good flesh that could be laying right here in the palm of old AJ's hands? I was determined to find out if she was swinging on the pole or licking the mustard jar. I tried everything from physically bumping into her in the cafeteria to volunteering for work after class in the newspaper office just to be close enough to strike when the iron was hot. It was like trying to strike Gold in a Silver mine. I was out of this girl's league but it wouldn't stop me from taking a shot at her fine ass.

Her ignoring me brought on an obsession that awakened all of the testosterone in my frail body. Every other girl on campus, black or white, practically took off their thongs when I walked by but not Reba. It was like dangling fresh meet in front of a wild animal, just having that perfect specimen of a woman anywhere within driving distance. Just getting a whiff of her body lotion sent my senses into orbit. Even when she spoke to me in that soft tantalizing voice, I would go around the corner and bite a hole in my damn lip like some fool instead of just grabbing her in one of AJ's lip lock specials. I wasn't going to allow any woman to set old AJ on his heels. I was going to be sure that she was receptive before making my patented move. My record was intact on never being refused and I wasn't about to have that broken by this perfect 10 or anyone else.

On campus, there is a pecking order. There are those who lead and can call their shots and those who follow and are more than willing to take what is left behind by the leaders. Up to now, I was one of the leaders . . . . I thought. No matter how good you think you are, there is always one son of a mother who was your nightmare. Shawn Samuels was the one guy on campus that could clean my clock in every sport but basketball but the white boy was brain dead when it came to the books. He was a tall, lean athletically build red bone with freckles wrapped around one of the meanest tempers imaginable. "We, on occasion, had a few run in but nothing serious until now. I was lucky that Shawn chose football over B'ball because I didn't like playing second fiddle to anyone especially a white boy who tried to identify black." Though I was nowhere near the physical specimen of Shawn, I was no slouch and didn't back down from any mother's son and you better believe that. It was not in my DNA to punk out but the time would come when I should have. It was like prison in the streets and if you punk out one time, the rest of the hood rats would have you for lunch, you can believe that.

College was as boring as high school but it didn't lack drama. In high school, the girls were just starting to grow their gardens and were all flirt and no action. Boys got their kicks from hiding under steps and checking out their Victoria Secrets. Once in college, girls started to allow a bit more loitering in their play grounds. Faye, a marble complexion heart breaker, who would stroll the campus as if she had her name on the mortgage, could cause a stir just by walking into a room. She has a medium build shapely frame with breast so firm that they caused you to lose control of your saliva glands. You couldn't help but focus on her cleavage, which seem to suck your eyes right out of their sockets. Her wardrobe consisted of nothing but mini dresses that hugged that ass like white on rice and stiletto heels which accented her shapely frame and killer legs to a point of making a brother loose his rocks from just looking at them. Her selection of outfits did not leave much to the imagination and my imagination blew up when she was within smelling distance. Even the male teachers would crash their old asses into something looking at that man-eating mamma-jama.

This girl was indeed fine and flirtatious and she realized the animal magnetism that she created just by her sexy walk. She could have any dude on campus including me but she had chosen Shawn because he could knock a hole in a steel plate and to cap it off, the sucker spent a fortune on her ass. She liked seeing him jealous to the point of leaving bodies scattered all over campus for just simply looking at her fine ass and usually she got what she wanted. Faye had her white play toy but there was no way Shawn could satisfy Faye. Hell, I don't know if anyone could but here is one brother that would die trying to tame that Tasmanian she devil.

Chapter V

The Beat Down

It was Thursday and a school day and I had to get to class on time. I woke to the smell of coffee, ham, eggs and home-made biscuits coming from the kitchen. "Yo . . . Moms, someone is doing some serious burning up in here. Did Aunt Doll come over or something cause I know you ain't burning like that?" A voice came from the kitchen, "the word is isn't AJ, not ain't. You are in college so act like it." "WELL Moms, since you put it like that . . . isn't that grub slamming up in here." "AJ, you are just wasting your time down at that college talking like that. That thug attitude plays right into the hands of those who want you to fail."

"Ah, Moms please just chill. I was just pulling your leg. I know how to use the queen's language when I need too. That's what gives us the edge Moms, don't you know that. "It's king's English not language, your vocabulary is stuck on stupid AJ." "Moms, we can adjust to whatever we need in order to survive." "Yea, I remember at registration just how much of an edge you had with . . . what was her name . . . . Ah, Ah Tanya. Have you seen her or spoken with her?" Yea, we are cool. I see her around campus." "August James, what happened to that confidence that you had with her at registration? She must have burst that male ego bubble of yours didn't she?"

"Mama please, I don't want to talk about Tanya. Why you bring her up anyway?" "Ouch . . . . I struck a nerve, ex-squeeze me Mr. Cool." Sometimes Moms could get on your last nerve and she knows how to stick your ass and twist the knife. She is my Moms but she was being a pain up in here. As I entered the kitchen still groggy and wiping the sleep from my eyes, Aunt Doll grabbed me in one of her patented bear hugs. She was a huge woman who had a heart as big as she was. "Aunt Doll, I knew it must have been you", I said while trying to catch my breath from being swallowed up in her jumbo sized tits. Things smelled too good and I knew Moms couldn't warm a roll in the microwave without burning it.

"AJ, are you still as afraid of the dark as you were when you were little", said Aunt Doll." "Aunt Doll just chill, you and Mama go around other folks talking that stuff." Say what you want, but Aunt Doll could cook some grub and would be often heard fussing with Mama about not giving Chantal a balanced meal before going to school. She would tell Mama that children need to learn on a full stomach. Her peach cobbler, mac and cheese, collard greens and crackling cornbread taste so good it will make you slap your Mama.

Now I know why when I go to the South to visit family and see all of the huge women, it's because they all eat like that down there. If you don't go back for seconds, it's an insult to them. If you have a somewhat thin frame like mine, they would say that you looked sickly. I don't know how healthy the food was being cooked in all that grease and all but it was the best I have ever had. The fried chicken, collard greens, mac and cheese, cornbread, fresh corn from the field and some of the best lemonade you ever tasted, will make your mouth water just smelling it.

I was 21 years old and still living at home with the parents for now but it was a complete drag and I will be in the process of getting my own place when my money was right. This college thing was cramping my style and I needed to make some money. I was in my sophomore year by now and college had been a long haul for me. Though my family was cool, I had to have my space and I couldn't do that without some serious money and my own crib. Basketball was my saving grace but I struggled in the off season. Occasionally I would go to Hyde Park for a pickup game but I had to make sure that it was somewhere out of the reach of Coach Boyd because he didn't believe in his players engaging in what he called "street ball." When you play in the hood you have to bring it or get embarrassed.

Moms' was tall and stylish and had a walk that definitely exposed her credentials. Her brown eyes, soft voice and big shapely legs drove Daddy crazy. He would always pretend that he was not the jealous type but he always kept one eye on the world and the other on Moms. Moms worked down town at Mable's Beauty and Nail Salon. Every woman in town who love the pampering scene, always found her way to Mable's. All of the world's problems were solved at the beauty salon or the barber shops in the black communities. "No matter how hard the work week had been, thing were made all right when you got to the beauty salon or barber shop." You may not have been able to solve the world's problems, but it helped to talk about them and there was always someone who was an expert at any subject that would come up. Most of these folks had not done well in life but could stroke their egos at the barber shop.

Pops had a decent gig as a restaurant inspector for the city of Chicago. He made sure that his work took him past the salon at least a couple times a day. I never understood why he was so insecure because Moms worshipped that dude and wouldn't tip with anyone for all the tea in China. Pops came home on time and brought his check with him. He never stayed out late with the boys because he had something to come home too. I was one to talk when Reba had inundated my mind constantly for the last month and I sure didn't want another dude tasting her cookies before I had a bite.

My Pops and I were never close. He was too busy making ends meet and keeping a good eye on Moms to give a shit about me. He never asked about school, never cared about how late I stayed out. I can't recall ever going to the park to throw the ball around or even go out in the empty lot to shoot baskets. The bonding thing was just out of the question. I felt like I was on my own anyway so I looked forward to the day that I could move out of their way. I had no doubt that Moms loved me but her drinking had gotten to a point no return and Daddy was too weak minded to do anything about it. Mom was one of those drinkers who could still perform even when she was soused. Nothing prevented her from getting to the salon because that was where she got all of the juicy gossip about all the movers and shakers and "the wannabe's" in the community.

My little sister Chantal was in the house so I had to mind my behavior because she was my main concern and if she was harmed in any way by their lifestyle I would never forgive them or myself. I wanted to get us both out of that apartment if I could. She was the prettiest little thing this side of creation. She was 13 years old, long brown pig tails, tall for her age with beautiful cat eyes and skin so perfect and smooth that it felt like a baby's behind. Chantal' had started to wear on me because she had started to blossom in all the right places and I knew sooner or later I was going to have to lay one of those hard heads out for trying to touch her up. She reminded me so much of Reba because it was all about reading, study and surfing the net on her lap top. If I needed any information for a report or parts for my car, she could find it on the internet. For a college dude, I was computer illiterate. Little pissant boys that think that she will be another notch on their belts, better have another think coming. I know that I can't watch her forever but before forever comes, they will have to come through me to get to her.

The night before, I could not get Reba out of my head. This girl had my mind all tied up in knots and that made me a bit uneasy. I had never before thought twice about any pair of fine legs so what made this set different. I had showered, put on one of my bitch catching shirt, a pair of designer jeans, my Jordan sneakers topped off with my brand new black Chicago White Sox cap. I was determined that day to impress Reba or die trying. I know she had noticed me but had too much uppity shit in her to recognize. There were opportunities to converse with her on my co-op assignments in the news room but my dumb ass blew ever chance with some dumb and stupid macho remark that didn't hit the mark with Reba *AT ALL*.

Though I had my old reliable 1992 Mustang parked in the garage, I preferred walking to school to save gas. I headed down Rose Avenue toward Fifty Third Street looking down at my every step to keep from scuffing my new Jordan kicks. As I reached campus headed for my 8:00 am class in macro economics, a voice came from Anderson Hall. "AJ, what's up? You're looking good enough to eat today my brother. Who are you trying to impress, me I hope?" Glancing to the left of the entry to the building was a shapely female standing in the shade of the doorway.

"No it couldn't be", I said to myself. After all, Faye had never given me the time of day. "Come here", the voice called out, "come closer so I can lay my eyes on your fine self." Finally I was close enough to see that it was Faye.

"What's up Fabulous Faye, you are finally giving a brother some play?" Proceeding cautiously toward the opening where Faye was standing, I perused the surrounding area hoping that Shawn the mauler was nowhere in sight. "Girl, where is your white night Shawn?" "What Shawn don't know surely want hurt him. I have been waiting to holler at you for some time now", was her response. "Girl, you are going to get both of us killed cause that crazy white cave man of yours loses his fricken mind when a brother get anywhere near your fine ass." "AJ, I never took you for a punk", come over here and give a girl one of those big hug cause you kicking it today my brother. I just want an innocent hug from you that's all, damn . . . why you trippin?" Are you afraid that your little woman Ashley will chap your young ass? Come on over here to Faye and get this hug that's waiting for you." Something told me to acknowledge her and keep pushing because I was late anyway. My ego wouldn't let me pass up a once in a lifetime chance to wrap my arms around a slice of Faye's heavenly pie.

As I reached to caress Faye and squeeze those melons of hers, she quickly placed her arms around my neck and pulled me so close to her that I could take her blood pressure. I could feel that strong heart beat . . . or was it mine? Before I knew it, she was sucking my face in a way that had me reminiscing about being on a warm beach sipping coconut rum in the Bahamas. I loved locking lips with that stallion because she was no amateur but I had to keep an eye out for Shawn. That white boy was hooked on that fine black meat. There is something to the old saying that if you ever go black, you will never go back and Shawn's ass was bitten by that black widow spider.

As I responded to her aggression, her tongue darted to the back of my mouth almost taking the little breath that I had left. By this time, my tool was so hard it almost pierced the silk mini dress that hugged Faye's body like warm soft icing on one of Aunt Doll's prize winning German Chocolate Cakes. Faye, feeling the effects of her body on my throbbing tool, smiled sensuously and asked, "Did I do that." Just as I was about to answer, out of the study hall walked Reba who sundered past us as if she wasn't even aware that we existed. Damn, of all the times for her to walk her fine ass by here. Did she actually see us or was she so focused and in her own world as she usually was? I was hoping that she was as focused as usual and didn't pay attention to what and who was around her as she usually does. I didn't want to blow a chance to be with Reba even for someone like Faye.

At that moment, Vickie, one of Faye's friends, approached and warned Faye that Shawn was heading in the direction of the study hall. "AJ, you better leave now but we will finish this later, if you can handle it", said Faye. As I was still trying to clear my head from Faye sucking every ounce of breath out of me and the near miss with Reba, I moved slowly toward Cameron Hall where my economic class was being held. I had completely lost track of time and was within 5 minutes of being late for old man Stinson's class. Realizing that Professor Stinson was no joke and hated tardiness, I picked up the pace to a slight jog. As I rounded the corner headed for the steps leading to my class, I bumped into, of all people, Shawn. "What's up AJ, in a hurry?" "Yeah man, just a bit late for class." "Cool, catch you later then'." Shawn and I were always casual with each other and indirectly realized that there was some type of competition going but it had never been a problem. We were in different sports and tended to run in different circles. He had no reason to suspect me of anything . . . . until now.

Shawn, looking back at me and me at him as I scurried away, headed in the direction of the study hall where Faye usually hung out between classes. As he approached the hall, he passed Keisha, one of Faye's posse members. "Hey, Keisha, have you seen Faye around? I was trying to catch up with her before my next class." "Yea, the last time I saw her she was talking with AJ and quiet as it's kept, you better watch that dude, he got his eyes on your prize, if you ask me. He was standing mighty close and the two was looking quite chummy to me if you know what I mean. See you later Shawn." Shawn, turned in the direction that he had last saw AJ as if to say, "Why didn't that punk mention that he had been talking with my woman?" When Shawn reached the study hall, Faye was nowhere to be found.

Shawn, known for losing it when Faye was in the mix, skipped the rest of his classed and parked himself at the entry to the campus knowing that both AJ and Faye would have to pass him headed home. All students would normally use the front exit to leave campus because the strip outside of campus had all of the burger joints and happy hour bars. After several hours of waiting on those cement benches, Shawn had worked himself up and was now pacing back and forth. It had to be 100 degrees in that quadrangle with all of the cement and Shawn had gotten himself so worked up that sweat had completely soaked his expensive silk shirt. In the state of mind that he was in, I don't think the heat mattered.

It was 4:00 pm and most classes were over and Shawn knew that it was only a matter of time before the crowd would pour out into the quadrangle. At a distance, Shawn could see Faye and her posse coming toward the entry as they normally did about that time. Keisha had failed to tell Faye of her conversation with Shawn and would regret the oversight. Faye, seeing Shawn, blurted out, "what's up baby, were you waiting on your better half?" Faye could see that Shawn was in one of those foul moods as he would normally get when she had pissed him off. "What's up Boo", she said, "what's wrong?" "I should be asking you what's up Faye. I heard that you been getting chummy with that dude AJ who you know I don't want around you cause he thinks he is big shit anyway. A.J and I are cool but not when it comes to my girl so what's up?" "Nothing's up and that was a few days ago when I was talking to AJ on the way to class, said Faye. "Why you lying Faye, Keisha told me that you and AJ was talking a few hours ago." If looks could kill, Keisha would be a dead ass posse member. Looking a Keisha, Faye said, "Keisha said what!!!!"

Keisha, knowing that payback from Faye would be hell, dropped her head and slowly slid in behind Freddy, another posse member. Keisha knew that a mistake like she had just made could cause her exit from the posse permanently. Those who in the past, had crossed Faye, had to leave the area or suffer the consequences from being ostracized to being discovered in some alley a victim of some unknown beat down. Though Faye was undoubtedly the queen of fine, she was also from the streets and was well connected with the sleaze factors and knew how to get things done without it tracking back to her. At that moment, I was approaching the group unaware that Shawn had found out about my little short escapade with Faye.

Shawn, seeing me coming, walked toward me and without saying a word, cold cocked me with a round house punch that Sugar Ray

Leonard would have been proud of. To make matters worse, as I tumbled backwards from the punch to the right side of my face, I just happen to have landed at the feet of who else but Reba, who again was just passing through the quadrangle on her way to the newspaper room. Now I knew what being in hell was like. On one hand, I had a big mouth full of Shawn's knuckle sandwich and on the other; I was embarrassed in front of Reba who I so terribly wanted to impress. I could see by vision of ever being with her going up in smoke. The game plan that I had crafted had just gone up in smoke.

Out of the corner of my now blacken and swollen eye, I could see Faye leaving with Shawn, still trying to convince him that nothing happened between her and me. As they moved away, Faye glanced over her shoulder and gave me a wink just to say, "I got power and I can do whatever the hell I want and get away with it." Keisha, knowing that she has crossed the line with Faye, came over to me to apologize. "AJ, my bad, I had planned to tell Faye about seeing Shawn but I forgot." "What did you tell that crazy dude anyway Keisha? You know how insane he gets at just the mention of Faye's name?" "I just told him that the last time I saw Faye she was talking to you, that's all." "Girl, that was enough to set that fool off and now I will have to face him again because I am not going to take this beat down without a pay back, that's the rules and even he knows it. Punking out is not an option Keisha, you know that. Apologizing to me are the least of your problems, you need to figure out how to deal with Faye." "I know, and what ever happened AJ, I just want you to know how sorry I am. Maybe I can make it up to you somehow. I mean, you know . . . . in any way you want me to . . . . any way."

"Can you believe this shit", I said to myself. Here I am lying on my ass and nursing a fat black eye and this girl is trying to ride my joy stick." Though Keisha ain't hard on the eyes, popping that was not high on my priority list. "Look, Keisha, you had better figure out how to deal with that crazy ass Faye. You know she is not going to let this go. You and I will settle up later." "Thanks for not being too upset with me AJ, I owe you big time." This was not the last that Faye and Shawn would hear from me, you can believe that.

I laid there on the grass for it seem like an hour, partly embarrassed and mostly feeling stupid for allowing Faye to make me one of Shawn's knockout victims. As I pulled myself together, I realized that it was my evening to work in the newspaper room with Reba. My day had gone from worst to disastrous. How do I face her with a swollen jaw, black eye and bruised ego? I could just go home and not help Reba but that's the coward's way out. I had gotten myself into this mess so not going to help Reba was not an option. "AJ, suck it up and face the music", I said to myself, "you got yourself into this mess so man up."

When I enter the news room, Reba was sitting at the desk using the computer to do the layouts for the next addition of the school paper. She briefly looked up at me and said, "Oh, hi AJ, I didn't hear you come in, there is a ton of things to get done today before the next issue comes out. I thought you were not coming seeing that you had a pretty busy day. I have to say you looked quite comfortable laying face down in the grass." I wouldn't have been that concerned about it had she not been smiling as if she was enjoying the moment. She acted as if she didn't notice all the damage to my mug.

The phone rang in the back office and Reba excused herself to answer it. After a few minutes of whispering, it seemed, she came back into the layout room. "AJ, that was my father that called and he is coming to campus. Would you mind walking with me and I can introduce you to him." "You bet your ass I would Reba." "AJ, why is it necessary for you to have such a foul mouth? You know I don't appreciate that mess." "OK, my bad Reba, I would love to meet your father." "Now, doesn't that sound a lot better", she said with a smile. "He will be here in a few minutes. I had asked if he would drop one of my books off to me that I left in his car earlier this week."

We waited a few minutes and started to walk toward the main entrance to the campus where we were to meet Reba's father.

Naturally I was curious about her parents because she had such a sultry and exotic look that there had to be some cross pollination going on. Her roots were from the big house not from the slave quarters. Old massa and Aunt Sarah met in the wee wee hours of the morning to start the process that eventually ended up producing this fine specimen of a woman. You know the massa had to have some of that dark meat every once in a while.

As we approached the entrance there was a curly haired, young looking white guy standing next to the flag pole. He was tall, approximately six feet two I would guest, lean and had that look of authority about him. As we got closer to the entrance, it seemed that he was smiling at us. No, this couldn't . . . . Before I could say another word, Reba rushed to meet him with a hug and kiss. "Thanks Daddy for bringing my book. It was a relief knowing that it was in your car. I thought that I had left it in one of my classes. Daddy, I want you to meet a friend who works in the news room with me. AJ, this is my father Dr. James Eckersley, Daddy . . . this is AJ." "How are you AJ? Any friend of my little girl is a friend of mine." I am losing my edge, it should have dawned on me that her father was white because when have you ever known a brother named Eckersley. I was so busy checking out the finer things in life and didn't even think about her last name. Now I am really wondering because her mom must be one fine black queen to have constructed the likes of Reba.

Man this guy must have had his clothes special cut for him because, I have to say, he was definitely representing. He had on a blue stripped Amana suit, accented with a blinding white shirt, gold silk tie and square to match. I couldn't help but glance down at his feet because the shoes usually set the look in perspective. If the shoes are not slamming, the rest of the package doesn't follow. It's like having a clean car with dirty tires or a thousand dollar suit with sneakers. He had on some black Italian gators shined to the max on top of some cold silk socks. I also noticed the diamond studded Rolex watch which sparkled like new money. His shirt collar and cuff had the initials DJE on them.

All of my suspicions about Reba were true. I knew she must have been a zebra. He was so prim and proper that he made me nervous and the dude had a grip like a vice for a slim dude. "Please to meet you sir", I said, feeling a little out of place and thinking that now I am really out of this girl's league. "So AJ, what are you majoring in?" I wanted to say, "Your daughter", but instead I said, "Business Admin Sir." "That's great AJ; Lord knows we need more good businessmen if you know what I mean. Have you thought about which Grad school you want to attend after undergrad?" I should have guessed that a dude like him would start "Truth or Consequences." Why is he asking all of these questions, I said to myself, and not once has he asked about the shiner that I had? "No sir, not yet but I will decide soon." "Well that's good AJ, maybe we can talk more about this later because I have to run to a conference across town."

As we shook hands and he kissed Reba goodbye, the one thing I was not looking forward too was another question and answer session with the doctor. It was as if he could look right through to my soul. As he approached the curb where a black town car was waiting, he quickly turned and in a very forceful voice said," Reba and AJ . . . . I am having a small dinner gathering on Saturday, why don't you kids drop by? It will give me an opportunity to continue our conversation AJ. See you there." Before we could respond, he had disappeared into the back seat of the limo. That had to be the longest fifteen minute conversation I had ever had. You would have thought that I had just asked for Reba's hand in marriage the way he was smoking me over.

I had no intentions of going to the dinner party until Reba brought it up again. "AJ, it would be nice if we could go by for a little while . . . . PLEASE???, ... it would make Daddy so happy. "Reba,

I would love to but not this Saturday." "Oh come on AJ, you are just trying to make up some excuse. I am counting on your going so that we don't disappoint Daddy, so what do you say." "Let me think about it Reba, you know all of this is so sudden and a man have to have a little air. Your dad was pressing hard and I don't want to have to play 20 questions when I get there. I will let you know tomorrow."

I could see that Reba was disappointed in my hesitance to go to her parent's home for dinner but her father made me uncomfortable and I don't really know why. It's definitely not because he's white because I suspected something was different about her from the start. Maybe it was because I was not sure where my college career was going and I didn't want to be pressed on the subject by her father. To accept the invitation would be stepping off into a world that I knew was deep water for me and I am not a great swimmer.

A slight mist of rain had started to blanket the area and I took the opportunity to pull Reba closer to me and cove her head with my light jacket. I don't know why but when things were over cased like this, it put me in a solemn mood. I could tell that Reba was appreciative of the gesture. "Thanks AJ; I really didn't want to get my hair wet, you know a girl has to keep her hair slamming." "Slamming", I said to myself. Is this the same Reba? She never uses slang. For the next few block of our walk back, things were quiet between us. As we got closer to the newsroom I couldn't help but ask, "Reba, what kind of a doctor is your father? He seems very nice." "He is a Cardiologist, and he is currently working on ways of eliminating the condition called enlarged hearts syndrome."

With every step I felt smaller and smaller in terms of dealing with Reba. Maybe I should stay with someone like Ashley. With her, I never had to be on the defensive as much as when I was with Reba. I felt that I was the authority with Ash but with Reba I felt that I should be sitting in a corner with a dunks cap on. "AJ, you seem to be in deep thought, what's up? If you are trippin about going to my parent's home, then don't do it." "Oh no, it's not that Reba, just thinking how impressive your father is. I can see a lot of him in you. He is accomplished, assured of his position in life, super confident." "AJ, what a nice thing for you to say! That was sweet. You try so hard to impress with that macho attitude but deep down inside, you are a teddy bear." "Well bears get a big hug so hug me Reba." "AJ, you got all of the hugs you are going to get on the walk back, my brother."

I knew that I had no intention of ever having dinner with her father and be grilled about my future. As we entered the newsroom Reba seemed in a great mood but had still not mentioned the beat down. I really wanted to taste that nectar but this brother was going to distance himself from this prime real-estate and today's events made me more convinced of that than ever. I had to figure out a way to get out of going to dinner without hurting her feelings.

As the evening wore on, her behavior was getting the best of me so I had to approach her about what had happened in the quadrangle. "Reba, speaking of what happened earlier today between Shawn and me, I am so sorry that you had to see my beat-down this evening. That dude cold cocked me when I wasn't looking. He surprised me and did not give me a chance to defend myself." "AJ, whatever happened between you and Shawn is between the two of you . . . . and Faye and doesn't involve me." She mentioned Faye in a very suggestive way of letting me know that she was paying more attention than maybe I gave her credit for. There was even a little movement of the neck as most black sisters will do when they are upset. Now, I am wondering just how much she really saw between Faye and me this afternoon.

"What do you mean Reba, what's Faye gotta do with this?" Reba snapped her head around as if to say, "AJ please." Her look made it obvious that she did see me sucking face with Faye, she must have or she wouldn't have said that. "AJ, what you do is your business but as quiet as it's kept, you got what you deserved. You knew already how jealous Shawn is about that floozy Faye but you were messing with her anyway", said Reba, obviously steamed by the conversation. She had responded as if it had struck a nerve. The easy going girl that I had just walked back with had become a neck moving, psychological, flame spurting adversary. Actually it was turning me on because that was her black side coming out and man did I love it. "Get your loins back in your britches AJ", I said to myself. But I couldn't back away from this fine girl who could get me to give up my player's card any day of the week by just asking. I wouldn't be myself if I didn't carry this a bit further because quitting now would always leave a question in my mind about what could have been. But there was still the question about going to dinner.

Reba seemed really upset when I brought up Faye. Was this an opening? Does she really care a little and just didn't want to admit it? Was that icy shell finally starting to crack? As we finished the evening, I did see a slight glance in my direction and just a hint of a smile. Maybe there was hope after all. Maybe if she did see what happened between Faye and me, it was somewhat of a turn on and old AJ just may be back in business.

I managed to slide right out of the dinner invitation by not seeing Reba or answering her calls until the following week. Even after I had flaked out on her the Saturday before, Reba seemed a bit friendlier toward me and we shared more of our personal situation with each other. I was careful not to screw it up this time so I am taking it slow and easy. Though she had on several occasions asked me to dinner with her folks, I would always have a conflict. I couldn't continue to refuse if I was to ever have a chance with her.

Chapter VI

Beat-Down Redemption

Now that I had started to get a foothold in a possible relationship with Reba, I couldn't help but think about the beat down that Shawn had laid on me and the smirk on Faye's face as they left me sprawled on the Northwestern Seal etched in the cement in the quadrangle. There had to be a way to get back at Faye without another run in with Shawn. Not only was Faye Shawn's girl, but that dude spent crazy money on her ass all the time. Who wouldn't get a little smoked if some other dude was wading in her pond? She had stepped out of line once before with a guy from Carver High and Shawn all but broke her face and the guy took such a beating that he had to leave school. It was the one and only time that he had laid his hands on her but it could be the opening that I needed.

Faye was flirtatious but she did not want to cross the line and risk the wrath of Shawn. I knew that she would often get her hair done on Thursdays around 5:00 PM at the shop where Moms worked. During that time, Shawn was usually working at Macy's Department store on the loading docks after class. The dude was a hustler and was making decent scratch, enough to keep Faye happy and I knew she didn't want to give up the meal ticket. His shift didn't end until after 10:00 pm which would give me plenty time to work the magic on

Faye. Faye was good but old AJ was a little better. I came from the same streets that she did so it was now my time to turn the tables.

It was Thursday evening of the following week and payback time. I drove my red 92 Mustang Convertible toward downtown passing The University of Chicago Booth School on North City front Plaza Drive and down along the Chicago River and parked a few streets over from the salon to wait for Faye to come out from her hair and nail appointment. After about a couple of hour in the chair touching up her hair and getting it fried, dyed and laid to the side, Faye strolled out wearing a short leopard dress, some pumps that stretched her frame another 5 inches and "bling" that sparkled with every sexy step. I allowed her to get several blocks from the shop so that I was not seen by my Moms who could blow my plans if she saw me. I also have to admit it was quite exciting following behind that fine piece of flesh with her hips giving you a sexual experience on the spot.

I followed at a distance for a while just to take in the motion of that backside ocean. The girl had it all and then some. I pulled up beside her and with excitement in my voice said," Miss, Faye with your fine self, it's AJ, what's up girl?" "AJ, you aren't still mad at me are you? You know a girl got to do what a girl got to do." "No doubt Faye but where are you headed now?" "Oh, just to do some more shopping before I go home. What's in that devious mind of yours, I can see devilish on your face AJ." "Girl, get in the car. I know a little burger joint on the river that is very secluded and you owe me that for that beat down anyway. You remember you promised to take up where we left off unless you didn't mean it or are you punking out like you told me." "AJ, I don't want any more trouble with Shawn and you shouldn't either." "Girl, like you told me, what Shawn don't know won't hurt him. I have as much to lose as you do. If Ashley sees your fine self getting into my ride, my ass is grass and she would be a Toro lawn mower. So get in girl, I will get you home before the dude gets off his gig, I promise."

Knowing that Faye has always lived on the edge, I knew she couldn't resist and quite honestly, I do believe there was chemistry if only sexual. "Ok AJ, I ain't playing with you, you better get me home before Shawn comes by my apartment. By the way I took care of Keisha's ass for ratting us out. That whore did that on purpose because she has always had a thing for Shawn. Her trifling ass thought I didn't know what a back stabbing bitch she was. What I did say was that her ass won't rat on me ever again, you can believe that." "Faye, what the hell did you do to that girl?" "AJ, quit asking questions and drive. What happened to Keisha is between her and me. Did you have a thing for Keisha AJ? I HOPE THE HELL NOT OR YOU CAN LET ME OUT OF THIS CAR RIGHT NOW." "Chill Faye . . . Damn . . . and quit raising your voice, I could have had Keisha anytime I wanted but why swim with minnows when you can ride around with the big fish." "Now you talking my type shit AJ, I didn't hurt the bitch just left her understanding what time it really is."

As I put a little pep in my step the phone started to ring. Now who can this be? As I flipped the mobil phone open, I could see it was Reba but how could I talk to her with Faye all up in my mug so I decided to let it ring. "Damn, AJ that is getting on my nerves, why don't you answer that thing or is it one of your ladies checking on you." "Quit trippin Faye, I got this. "Hello." "Hello AJ, what are you up to? I just thought maybe we can hang out before I have to go to the library." "Oh, that is a nice suggestion but I can't right now but I will call you back later OK, Goodbye." As I glanced over at Faye, she had this smirk on her face and was not buying the vanilla discussion that I just had. "AJ, you are a trip. Who was she?" "That was just a friend of mine Faye so what's the big deal?" "You are straight out lying and the truth ain't in you. You could have talked to whoever she is, I'm cool." "It must have been your little nookie Ashley, checking on your young ass or was it that Reba chick that you almost fainted over her seeing us sucking face that day at the library?" "AJ, just handle your business." Man I get tired of these bitches reading me like some used book. The luster is definitely leaving the game and I can't afford to have that happen. Since when have the hunter been captured by the game."

My timing was wack, and I again had given up another opportunity to hang out with Reba. I was slowly coming to the realization that Reba and I weren't on the same wave cycle. Every time she had made the effort to spend time with me, I had my head in the proverbial sand like now. I am in this thing to win it so there was absolutely no way I was going to let Fay out of my grasp. This thing between us is coming to a head one way or another.

As we drove toward the river and Lake Shore Drive, I couldn't help glancing over at her legs which were very visible and the leopard dress was so short that I could almost see her sunshine." AJ, you must see something you want." Faye was quite aware of what I was doing as played alone by moving her hips side to side with the beat of Barry White's song, *Practice What You Preach*, which was totally appropriate. It goes like this. *"Girl, there is something wrong with me, cause every time I'm alone with you, you keep talking about you loving me. Hay Babe, your foreplay just blows my mind, so why don't we stop all this talking girl, why don't we stop wasting time. I've had my share of lovers, some say I'm damn good, and if you think you can turn me out, baby I wish that you would, cause you keep telling me this, and telling me that, and once I am with you I can never go back. "All I can tell you tell you Miss Faye is you may have to practice what you preach."*

"Barry said it better than I could Faye. I tell you baby girl, if you ever get a piece of old AJ, you will throw rocks at Shawn and you can believe that. I do practice what I preach and you better believe that." Faye just smiled and kept moving to the music getting me all greased up. "Boy if you had some of this you wouldn't live to tell about it", she shot back. "I ain't found a sucker yet who can really handle this, including Shawn. Shawn is just a means to an end, if you know what I mean. He is well connected and can get a girl what she needs. He is all right but he can't feed my mo Joe baby boy and I doubt if you can either." Man this hammer was trippin, I would give that thing a black eye, put a seven inch gash in her cerebellum and definitely make that liver quiver and you can believe that.

Barry's words just served to fire me up more and increase my expectations. It was time for her to put up or shut up. Faye had talked a good game so now it's time to get on the score board. We arrived at the burger joint and spent the next hour taking in the scenery. The restaurant was strategically placed overlooking the most scenic part of the lake. It was the perfect setting to test my assumption about Faye that of seeing if she was as interested in testing me sexually as I was in testing her. We had two pitchers of beer and some of those little fish looking cheese crackers and I could see that Faye was getting a slight buzz. I didn't have much money in my pocket so I was hoping that she would fill herself with the crackers and beer and not want to order anything else. Faye had a big appetite and that big girl could throw down some grub but she seemed happy munching on the crackers and beer.

I was sitting directly across from Faye when all of a sudden I could feel her foot slowly rubbing the inside of my leg which was causing immediate hard feelings if you know what I mean. I could see that it was turning her on as much as it was me. As she moved up my leg and was rubbing my tool with her foot, she was licking her lips inviting me to come along. "All right girl, you are playing with fire now you better believe that." She shot back, "either you got more fuel to fan these flames or are you going to pour water on it little man. This fire will burn your ass if you don't handle it carefully." Now this big hammer is pushing my button and it's like the streets, I can't punk out now. She will be calling me Big Man after I knock the roof off that sucker.

It was part of the plan to selected this place because upstairs were rental rooms which made my plan that much easier. I asked Faye to excuse me for a minute and that I would be back shortly.

I had already rented a room hoping that Faye wouldn't reject me and my invitation. As I approached the front desk, one of the white guys on the desk recognized me. "You are AJ and you play for Northwestern don't you?" "Yea man, you must have seen one of my games." "Yea, right", said the desk clerk. This was a little strange that this dude recognized me. What I didn't know was that he was a friend of Shawn's and his seeing me would start another string of incidents with Shawn that was destined to happen anyway.

After checking to see if the room was ready, I returned to the patio where Faye was sitting and could see that the beer was kicking in and the girl was ready for just about anything. "AJ, where were you. You can't leave a sister sitting alone for such a long time. Some of the guys sitting over by the window would love to take your place she said with a sexy lip licking smile. "The best thing they can do is admire from a distance and go and whack off because there is nothing over here for them and you can bet on that. "Now come on girl, I want to show you something." I reached for her hand and slowly pulled her toward me. Faye said with a sheepish look on her face, "are we leaving AJ? I am not ready to go." With a smile and a wink I was about to lead this fine ass sheep to the slaughter.

I had vision of that day when she and Shawn had walked away from me after the beat down and now pay back was going to be a bitch. As we strolled past the desk, Alex the desk clerk who had spoken to me was standing behind the door to the back office. What I didn't know was that he had seen Faye sitting on the patio and didn't want to be recognized because Faye would have identified him as a friend of Shawn. I was also to find out later that this little evening get together would not be unknown to Shawn.

We arrived at the room which was 119 which happen to be 911 backwards. Like 911, this was shaping up to be one of those situations that will remain with me for a long time and represent a life changing experience. Once inside the room, it was obvious that

Faye had been a key participant in this script many times before. I had a dime bag of weed in my pocket and what a great way to set the mood. I had said that I was going to keep away from the weed for a while but I had to use every tool in my bag to get a saddle on this stallion. "Hey Faye, let's take a hit off of some of this good stuff and take in the scenery." The room had a view of the balcony that was no less than spectacular. I quickly lit a joint and took a long and satisfying drag, closed my eyes and let the aroma tickle my nostrils. Faye, instead of taking her own drag, placed her lips over mine to share my portion. It surprised me but was more than welcomed. The smell of her perfume, her soft wet lips and the smell of the weed sent us both to another level. It was no doubt in my mind now what was about to happen.

The room was tastefully decorated with a double bed, a mini bar, ceiling lights, a large mirror which would come in handy as I moved deeper into the moment. "His" and "hers" robes was hanging by the door which gave the room a little taste. In the bath area was a tub and a shower head that looked like something from outer space. The radio next to the bed was playing soft Jazz and 2 mints lay on the lamp table on the right of the bed. The bed spread and curtains were a pale yellow which accented the very appropriate wall paintings of scenes in Italy and colorful rugs were arranged throughout the room. To the right of the bed stood a stand and bucket with some cheap champagne and two glasses. Not bad for a boy from the projects even though Moms was paying for all of this. If she knew how I was using her money, I would be cut off for good. I may not have had much scratch in my pocket but I knew how to impress. In order to get the best, you have to give the best.

"Look Faye, let's sit here for a minute and continue to enjoy some of this good stuff." Each time I took a hit from the weed, she would place her lips on mine. Her lips were soft and tender and tasted sweet as if she had just consumed a bouquet of sweet roses. This hamma was hot as a firecracker and carried twice the explosive.

After taking a few more drags off of the weed, Faye wasted no time in taking my hand and placing it on those fine melons and pulled me into her web just as she had done on campus. After a moment of teasingly running her hand up the inseam of my trousers, she stood up and started to slowly unzip her dress. I sat on the edge of the bed taking it all in. First the dress dropped slowly to the floor exposing a red braw that barely covered her nipples and a red g-string that was smoking from the fire between her legs. I started this as a payback but now I am wondering if I knew what the hell I was getting myself into. This woman was so fine it was scary. She had curves in places that most girls didn't have places. That body of hers was built for speed and endurance and I was about to find out how fast and how long I could hang with this girl who had a body by Fisher and a mind by Mattel. My reputation was at stake and I had to represent.

While she was doing her mating dance for me, I had quickly removed my trousers getting ready for the main event. She asked me to lie back on the bed and let her take me to a place I had never been before and I was more than happy to oblige. For the first time in my life, I have to admit that I was unsure of myself. What if I couldn't keep up with this stallion? What if she turns me out? How could I face anyone on campus if Faye dogs a brother out? She is the type that will tell on your ass if you can't step up to the plate. I was hoping that I had brought my "A" game because from the looks of what was standing in front of me, I would need an "A Plus."

Her hands began to explore my chest my stomach and in one motion, he tongue started to caress my belly button in a circular motion while removing my shorts. This was a pro and I was now in up to my neck and it was too late to back out now though I was beginning to think that it would be in my best interest to do so. With each circular motion of her tongue she would start sucking my navel until my tool sprung up like a jack in the box.

Things were moving so quickly that it could have ended this episode as swiftly as it had started. My entire body was shaking.

I couldn't allow her to continue down this road because it would be over before I could even start. The volcano was starting to boil much too quickly. She finished pulling my shorts over my throbbing tool and went to work on it as she had done to my belly button. She seemed pleased and shocked at the size of my tool but wasted no time in totally consuming it and sending me into a state where I actually thought that I was losing my frickin mind. As her warm tongue caressed and enveloped my manhood, my legs and lower body seemed numb as I was slowly but surely losing control of being in control.

I removed her bra to expose two of the most beautiful twins a woman could have. Her nipples were firm and standing at attention like two soldiers saluting the flag. She straddled me pulling aside her G string preparing to guide my tool in her hot oven. I had to take control or this woman was going to cause a gusher before I was ready so I forced her over on her back and spread her legs so wide that she gave out a loud moan as I entered her from the back. She seemed shocked at my sudden aggressiveness. I do pride myself on my attributes and she was about to get all of what old AJ could give. As I forced my tool in her hot enclave, she gripped the sheets so hard that she pulled them from under the mattress. I knew then that I was in the game. I pumped her harder and harder until she pleaded for me to stop. There was no stopping me now because I wanted to give her some of the medicine that I am sure that she had dished out to many unfortunate brothers who could not tame this Brahma Bull. As I thrust deeper and deeper into her wet rose garden, she gave out grunts that were so sensual that I couldn't help cry out in ecstasy with her. I tried my best to hold out and extend the episode of the best sex I ever had until she regained control by started to shiver all over. She started to shake her body with such passion that we both tumbled to the floor still locked in each other embrace and still mixing our potions. We both grunted and groaned so loud that anyone in the adjoining room must have heard us, but who cared at that point. Faye yelled out my name and moaned in a manner that let me know that I had her at the top of the mountain and she was about to take the leap as we both hit the climax ceiling at the same moment right there on the carpet.

I had experienced some heavy love making in my young life but nothing had ever taken me to this level. We were both soaked with our body juices and laid exhausted after about 30 wonderful minutes of sexual combat. It was the first time that I could remember that Faye was totally silent. We laid there for it seemed like hours on the rug without saying a word just staring at the ceiling. Faye had her head on my chest and her legs wrapped around mine in a manner or resignation. We both had to know that this was going to be a problem. You don't have sex at this level and make it a onetime deal but I wasn't ready to tempt fate and chance facing Shawn again but I knew this wasn't over by any stretch of the imagination. There would be another time for me and Faye, and I looked forward to it. I didn't care anymore about getting back at her for the beat down because she had lived up to her reputation. Old AJ had truly represented and you can believe that. We laid there for it seemed like hours though only for a few minutes just enjoying the moment and smelling the aroma of our great love making session.

We glanced at the clock by the bed and both realized that it was only an hour before Shawn would be off work and headed to Faye's apartment as he would normally do. We gazed deeply into each other's eyes and without hesitation were again locked in each other's embrace as hot and heavy as the first time. This time she straddled me in the sitting position and in one motion had mounted me again with the force of a jack hammer. Her thrusts were so hard and sensual that it brought me to a climax instantly and I gave out a holler that just pierced the quietness of the room. I rolled her off just to get my breath. By this time another 30 minutes had passed and it would take some time to get dressed and at least 25-30 minutes to drive to Fay's crib.

As we dressed to leave, Faye remained quiet and reserved and I tried to rejuvenate her by reminding her of the time and our need to get back before Shawn gets off. It was 8:00 pm and Shawn would be getting off the clock in about 30 minutes. He would only have about a 20 minute drive to Fay's place giving us just enough time to freshen up a bit and head to her place. For the first time, Faye didn't seem that concerned about the time or about Shawn. It concerned me though because I could always cover my flanks during the day but at night, it was a little shaky and sometimes unnerving.

As I pulled up to Faye's apartment building, she slowly moved her head and eyes toward me before she said, "ok AJ, what now, I really don't know what happened but I need to see you again?" I got out of the car without a response and went around to the passenger side to let her out. I returned to the driver's side and with a slight grin, I left her with the same look that I had gotten at the beat down that said, "I got the power now and I can do whatever the hell I want and get away with it." I had given Faye some of her own medicine but why didn't I feel good about it. I believe that she had made as much an impact on me as I had on her. There would be a sequel to this day, you can bet on it.

I quickly hurried to get into my car and had started to pull away when a Silver Lexus pulled in front of me and out of the passenger seat stepped Alex, the clerk that had seen me at the hamburger joint. Had he seen Faye too? From the driver side stepped Shawn dressed in tight jeans and a body shirt that displayed every ripple in his perfectly sculptured 220 pound body. I knew then that Shawn had gotten the down low on what had happened between Faye and me. Stepping out of the car with his hands above his head, Shawn stated, "AJ, here we are again dude, and with my girl again." Faye, knowing what Shawn was about to do, jumped between Shawn and me and began to explain that I had picked her up down town and was bringing her home and that was all. Shawn, without thinking, slapped Faye with the back of his hand knocking her to the ground.

"Faye, you are a lying sack of shit and I am tired of putting up with your crap, I don't need your ass anyway. I know you and this dude was knocking boots down by the river. My posse is all over and your ass can't hide. I treat your ass like a queen and this is my pay back?"

Seeing Shawn slap Faye brought out the Rambo in me. Without even thinking, I bum rushed Shawn grabbing him by the shoulder and as he turned, I put all of my 185 pounds into a punch that sent him stumbling against the car. Knowing that he was only temporarily dazed, I quickly move to the back seat of my car to get a hickory stick that I kept for dogs. I was not about to take another embarrassing beat down and I was not going to allow him to whip up on Faye like that. As Shawn turned around preparing to retaliate, I stepped toward him with the stick and swung it so hard that it gave off a sound that startled him and his posse. The force of the swing stopped him cold in his tracks.

For the first time, Shawn ended up on the short end of my beat down and I was confident that if he wanted some more of old AJ, it was there for the taking. Shawn looked at me and at Faye, who was still lying on the side walk dazed from the slap, pointed his finger at the both of us and ran his finger across his throat as if to say we were dead meat before jumping into his car and speeding away. I knew it wouldn't be the last I would hear from that dude but the dye had been casted.

"AJ, I am so sorry to have gotten you into this again. How did he know we were together anyway?" "That Punk Alex, who was riding with him, I saw him at the hotel when we were there. You didn't see him when we passed the front desk and I didn't know that he was Shawn's friend. Faye, you are too good a person to put up with that dude. Any chump who would hit a woman is a coward and don't deserve your company." "You got that right AJ but it will be hard for me without Shawn's help. I can't afford this apartment on my own." "Well Faye, as I see it, you got a choice of either continuing to be his doormat or holding your head up and figure it out on your own. Girl, you have a gift for design just look at you. I will talk to my friend Andre' and see if he can use your skill in his dress shop on 5th and High." "Would you do that for me AJ after all of the problems that I have caused you?" "Sweet lady, after the time that you and I had today, that is the least I can do."

I took my thumb and rubbed a slight tear away as I cupped her face in my hands. You are indeed a special woman who deserves to be treated with dignity and respect. This was bound to happen between Shawn and me. It was just a matter of time. I just hate that you had to be in the middle of it." "Thanks AJ, that's the nicest thing that anyone has ever said to me. You make me feel special not because of how I look or my figure but because you see me, the person and I appreciate that more than you know."

I gave her a slight kiss on one jaw and then the other and turned to leave when Faye grabbed my arm and asked, "what now AJ?" You have truly rocked my world in more ways than one so what now?" With a wink and a smile, I left Faye pondering the answer. I knew it wouldn't be the last I would see of Faye but I had to have my space for a while. Faye is like that potato chip commercial, you can't just have one and not want more. She had just made it that much harder for the other women in my life. There was not a chance that I would past up another day like this with Faye, not a chance.

It was Friday now, and the last day of the semester and another opportunity to spend the evening with Reba in the news room as we approached the end of the semester. No matter the great time I had spent with Faye, I was determined to get a final break through with Reba and this was the day. Reba walked in wearing a pair of designer jeans that showed every curve on her well sculptured body. She, though not quite as sexy as Faye, could turn heads by simply walking into a room. Down the side of the jeans was the word perfect and written across the chest of her black sequenced blouse was the word Jesus Treasure. It was the first time that Reba had allowed this more tantalizing side of her to show. I was like Ex President Jimmy Carter; I was committing sin all over the place in my mind. Was Reba dressing like this to impress me? I would like to think so. After all she showed the sensitive side the other day. Did she feel that she needed to dress a little more provocative to be in the game? I hoped so.

As the evening wore on, I found myself daydreaming about the evening with Faye but Reba had also noticed my preoccupation. "AJ, why are your eyes so red and you seemed pre-occupied", what's up?" "Oh nothing Reba, just a little tired today". I could use a little company after work, just don't feel like going home right away. There is a little Deli not too far from here and I would be honored if you would share a sandwich and cup of coffee with me." "Wow AJ, since you say it that way, how can I refuse. What's gotten into you, being so polite and all?" "OK Reba, give a brother a break, you are so use to seeing the ghetto side of a brother that you have never noticed that old AJ can be quite a catch."

"AJ, you seem like a really nice guy but it's obvious to me that you are doing some type of drug because your eyes are red and glassy all the time." I will go but you have to promise that you are straight up and not messing with that stuff while you are around me." "Reba, I do some weed at times but what's wrong with that?" It may be ok to you but it wrong for me and I want no parts of it", Reba shot back. "OK, OK Reba, I'm straight and I haven't had a smoke for a long time" . . . "By the way AJ, aren't you dating someone named Ashley? Why not have her meet you for a bite to eat and Lord knows you seem to have the hots for that Faye person so why not her?" How did Reba know about Ashley and here she go again with that Faye stuff? I never once mentioned Ashley to her so how did she know? This woman must be working for CSI Chicago or something.

"Ah! Reba, Ashley and I are just good friends and we go out sometimes but nothing serious. You know that a man has to have a little female companionship from time to time and you wouldn't give a brother the time of day." "AJ, between Faye and this Ashley person, you don't have time for me but that's OK, we can still have a bite to eat." Now I am really puzzled. How long has she known about Ashley and it's evident that she is not a fan of Fabulous Faye?

After having a great evening with Reba, something was missing. As much as my whole existence was geared to getting Reba to notice me, now it seems somewhat anticlimactic. Had my brain and loins been fried by the mind blowing sexual encounter with Faye? Had my attempt to get back at Faye for the beat down by Shawn backfired on me? Whatever it was, I had to find out quickly or once again blow this obvious opportunity that seems to be staring me in the face with Reba.

Since Faye had started to work at the dress shop, we had many more encounters. The thing that I liked about Faye was that she was a lot like me in that she wanted it when she wanted it and did not put any pressure on a brother. I had started limiting my time in the newspaper room after school because the summer was approaching and I didn't have quite the desire to get a notch on my belt with Reba since I was spending so much time with Faye. How I managed all of this without pissing Ashley off, I don't know. Ashley had a very demanding schedule which allowed me to have quite a bit of free time. Many times, she was satisfied just getting a call from me after work because she was usually tired.

Just as that thought cleared my mind, the phone rang and it was Ash. "What's up Ash?" "Oh nothing AJ, why don't you come by tonight and I will fix you a great dinner who knows what your desert will be. I am feeling the need for a little TLC big boy, it's been a while." That's was definitely not what I needed after having another round with Faye just yesterday. "Ok, Ash, it will be around seven before I can get there." "That's fine with me as long as I see you." Now what was I going to do? I didn't have the energy to go another round with anyone after the mind and body draining sex with Faye. I couldn't let Ash down though because she has my back no matter what.

I decided to stop by the gym on my way home to try and work up an appetite for Ash's meal. Ash was not known for her cooking but she could get by. I could expect some corn on the cob, black eyed peas, corn bread and some Lee Roy the barn yard pimp. Ash could eat chicken every day.

Pumping iron gave me a degree of release from the world. It allows me to recharge my batteries after a long day. It clears my mind and the musty scent challenges me to push much harder to clear my lungs of the bad habits that creep into my world from time to time. Seeing the ladies with the skin tight work-out clothes usually causes my testosterone levels to rise but not this time. I took my precious time getting home to change before going to dinner with Ash.

I arrived at Ash's apartment at exactly 7:00p.m. Before I could knock on the door, Ash as if she was clairvoyant, opened it before my hand hit the wood. She must have been standing at the window watching for me. "Hello AJ, I have missed you." "Missed you too Ash." "Wow AJ, I would have expected a little bit more than 'me too Ash' since it's been a while since we last spent some quality time together." "You are right Ash, I just have had a lot on my mind lately with school and all and not having found a job yet for the summer." Come on in the kitchen with me AJ while I finish dinner. As we strolled through her apartment which was always immaculate, I could not help noticing the well placed table set up, the wine glasses and her finest china. Ash had a lot on her mind over and above the dinner. She was wearing a tight fitting dress, one that I always loved to see her in. Though she did not possess the perfect ten body of Faye or Reba, she used what she had well and I truly loved being in her company. I was involved with three different women, all having different strengths. With Faye, it was totally sex; with Reba, it was class and with Ash, it was support and security.

Everything was leading to a night of high expectations on Ash's part that I would be in a romantic mood. As she put the dinner on the table she had this inquisitive look on her face. "AJ, you have been here for over an hour and you have not kissed me as you usually do. What's wrong? Are you seeing someone else?" "No, no Ash, I am just tired tonight, haven't been sleeping well lately." "Well after dinner, I want you to go up to the bed room, take a hot bath and I am going to give you the best message that you have ever had. How does that sound?" With a smile and a wink, I said, "Sounds great Ash, I could use a good rub down and a little shut eye." "AJ, I will put you to sleep alright." I knew what that meant and I was not sure that I was up to it.

I took my time downing what was a pretty impressive dinner and after a couple of glasses of Starmont Chardonnay, I was feeling somewhat revived and I have to admit, Ash was my favorite in bed until I was introduced to the major leagues by Faye. As I took my last bite of food, I noticed that Ash had taken her hair down and was looking pretty seductive. She lit two candles, came to the end of the table where I was sitting, slightly pulled up her dress just enough to allow her to straddle me, placed her face on my shoulder and set quietly for what seemed to be hours. She was happy just having me there. Now I am feeling worst than if I had not been able to perform up to standard. She was really what I needed but greed had caused me to want more. More of what, ... I do-not-know.

Ash, had dropped off into a deep sleep. I slowly eased her up, placed her comfortably in my arms and carried her to the bedroom where I undressed her to her panties and bra and covered her very comfortably. As I stood staring at her before I let myself out, a serene feeling came over me causing me to crawl in bed next to her and lay quietly just enjoying the quietness of the night and her body laying so peacefully. Though I never got my promised massage, I was spared of having to perform under less than perfect conditions.

This particular evening was a blessing in disguise because I really did have need of a good night sleep. Morning came somewhat quicker than I had expected. I looked over at Ash who was still in a deep sleep. I took a sheet from her note pad and left her a short note. "Ash, thanks for one of the best nights I have had in a long time. Even though I never got my massage, I am sure I'll have a rain check. I did spend the night and had one of my best nights of sleep for a long time. Thanks for a great dinner. See you soon sweetheart. I still owe you and I know you understand what I am referring to (smile)."

Chapter VII

The Summer Months

The end of the school term was finally here and I knew this would be my last semester even though I had another two years to finish my degree in Economics. I was destined for the unemployment line for the summer while Reba was headed for her law classes at Harvard Law School. Reba was two year ahead of me in school and slowly but surely moving out of my life. Reba had not allowed me to even smell that nectar and now she was about to leave Chicago for the sophisticated shores of the Ivy League. Surely those brothers without the mind clutter that I suffer from will be able to finally get through that tough exterior of hers. I have to look at it as the one that got away.

As the summer months rolled by, I didn't see much of Reba because she was busy taking law courses preparing for her entry into law school. I was on my way to the dairy queen with Chantal when I received a call from Reba. Her message was that she would be leaving Chicago on Monday and that she wanted to say goodbye. Why was I kidding myself, Reba was well beyond my reach. Why spend the time saying goodbye to her when there was a great possibility that it would be the last time I would lay eyes on her.

Against my better judgment, I agreed to meet her at the airport. After all, she had been a great friend and I really enjoyed her company without there being any physical contact. Being late as I usually am, I figured that Reba would have gone through security because there was only 45 minutes until her flight was to leave.

As I approached the ticketing area, Reba called to me. "AJ, over here, hurry or I will be late. I didn't want to leave without saying goodbye." "Thanks Reba, I will miss you, go on over to the Ivy League and make us proud." "I will miss you also AJ but just one thing you should always remember, don't make assumptions because they may be wrong. You should go after what is important to you, if you know what I mean." Maybe, at some point, I would understand what she meant by that statement.

With that, Reba kissed me on each jaw and with both hands on my face, kissed me tenderly like I had dreamed of for a long time. Her lips were so soft and sweet that they reminded me of the Crispy Cream donuts when they come right out of the oven. They just melt in your mouth. I was standing there as if I didn't know what to do. Why was I so shy with her after she had given me signs that she cared? "AJ, we will see each other again, I promise", said Reba as she walked toward security. She had a look of really not wanting to leave and for some reason I was paralyzed and acting as if it meant nothing to me. As she disappeared into the corridor of the plane, I suddenly realized that the opportunity that I had waited for such a long time had walked out of my life and into a world more fit to her pedigree.

I spend the first weeks of the school break looking for employment. Man it was tough out there and I needed some quick cash. As I was leaving the beauty shop where Moms worked, a black Mercedes 500SL pull up beside me and the tented window rolled slowly down and a booming voice pierced the air. "What's up AJ? It's been a long time my vanilla wafer brother." I stooped to see who was in the back seat and low and behold, it was Cat Daddy, I hadn't seen him since high school. "What's up yourself Cat, you are rolling large these days my well dressed brother. It seems that you have done something right or . . . . wrong." Cat just peered out of the dark backseat with a smile worth solid gold. It fact his grill was solid gold." Brother AJ, what I do at night allows me to roll big during the day. I am in Human Resources, my inquisitive friend. I am in the people business, ha, ha, ha." I decided to let things lay just where they had fallen. The dudes surrounding him were definitely not his personal secretaries and the heat on their belts did give me an idea of what business he was in. "Look AJ, the word on the street is that you are looking for a gig while you are out of your precious college, is that true?" "Ah, yes but I am cool." "Listen AJ, we were always tight and I want to help a brother out. I have a little job I want you to do for me. When it's over, there are ten big ones in it for you. What do you say?" "What kind of job commands that type scratch Cat?" "Look AJ, you don't even have to know any details, I just need you to take this little box to the Makline building on 24th and put it in the hands of a guy by the name of David Sorenson. His office is on the 5th floor. As you get off the elevator, turn right and go straight to the back of the building. You will see a set of double glass doors. Go through them and his office is on the right." "May I ask who this David Sorenson is?" "YOU MAY NOT, now do we have a deal of what?" If you decide not to take the 10K, I will get it done AJ. I just wanted to help a friend in need."

I knew this did not smell right but ten big one could give me a little independence and a way out of mom's and Dad's space. "AJ, I don't have a lot of time, what's the word?" OK, ok . . . give me the package and I will make the drop. I am doing this for old times Cat." "I knew you would help and old friend AJ. Now when you make the drop, call me at this number." The thug sitting in the front seat handed me a card with the number to call. The building was just two blocks over and in walking distance. As I walked slowly North on Ventura Avenue, my stomach was turning in knots knowing that something wasn't right. Why couldn't he make the drop himself? What was I getting myself into? I knew this was wrong so why was I doing this?

As I walked into the Makline Building, an eerie feeling came over me but I had committed and I was going through with it. It seemed as if everyone knew what I was there for because they seemed to focus on me . . . or was it my imagination getting the best of me. I proceeded to the elevator, pressed the button for the 5th floor and the ride seemed an eternity. As I looked for the double glass doors, my nerves were getting the best of me. Half way down the hall, I stopped. Sweat was popping off my brow as if I had just come in out of the rain. "Get it together AJ", I said to myself. "Just walk in, identify Mr. Sorenson, drop the package and be gone." As I walked into the office, the secretary asked whether I had an appointment." "No I don't, but I wanted to drop this package off to Mr. Sorenson, I think he is expecting it." "Ok, I will take it." "In all due respect, I have to deliver it to Mr. Sorenson." Without further argument, she got on the phone. "Mr. Sorenson, there is a man here with a package for you." "Thanks Sherri, I will be right out." As Mr. Sorenson, took the package, two men dresses to the nine's came out of his office and took the package. Mr. Sorenson was part of a drug sting operation to identify the source of what proved to be a sophisticated Meth ring operating in the area and there I was caught up in it with no place to go and no explanation of my involvement. "Young man, please step into the office", said one of the detectives. Once in the office, he started by saying, "make it easy on yourself and tell us your source." "Sir, I don't know what you mean, I was asked to deliver a package to Mr. Sorenson and that's what I did." "You always drop packages off for people without asking questions?" "No sir, I know this individual and I was doing him a favor." "Well, young man, he didn't do you any favors. "Who is the person that asked you to drop off the package?" I knew that was going to be the next question. If I tell, I get Cat in trouble, and if I don't, I am subject to be arrested.

"Sir the only thing that I can tell you is that we call him Cat. I am not sure what his real name is, we have called him Cat since we were kids." "Do you know where he lives?" "No sir, we just would hang out together when we were in high school." "Young man, this package contains some of the most powerful Meth on the street. We are going to have to take you down to the station until you can give us a little more than you are giving."

Now what do I do? I was not about to give them the number that Cat had given me but I can't take the hit for this. He got me involved in something that I knew had to be wrong but I did it anyway. They spared me the embarrassment of handcuffing me but I was going to be booked never the less. I had one call per the law and I was going to call Cat.

After booking was complete, I was asked if I wanted to make a call. They moved me into a small room with a phone and a table and 2 chairs. They had not asked me to empty my pockets so I still had the card from Cat. I dialed the number and it rang and rang with no answer. Finally, Cat answered. "What's up AJ, did you take care of business for me?" "Cat, I am in jail, you got me caught up in a sting man, what am I gonna do?" "Shit AJ, how the hell did that happen?" Evidently, they have been watching Sorenson and they may be watching you." "AJ, what did you tell them man?" "I told them that you asked me to drop off a package and that's all I knew." "Did you give them my name?" "No I didn't, because I don't even know your name. That's why I am down here. They think I am a part of some drug ring. Please tell me that you are not involved in drugs Cat."

"AJ, I am so sorry man. I didn't intend for this to happen. Give me time to figure this out." "Yea, but in the mean time, I am stuck here. What am I going to tell my parents?" At that point, the phone went dead. "I am, not worried so much about tonight because my parents know that I often stay over at Ash's place but what happens tomorrow? As I hung up the phone, the detective came in to see if I could give them any more information. After telling them that I had told them all that I knew, I was led to a cell where I stayed until the next morning.

I paced that little small cell all night. I didn't get a wink of sleep. At about 7:00 am, the detective came in and told me that I was going to be allowed to leave because a man had come in and admitted giving me the package. The man's name was Cecil A. Turner. As I walked through the booking room, I saw CAT sitting with 2 officers. He looked over and acknowledged me with a head nod. CAT had turned himself in to get me out of this mess. Though I had dodged a direct hit, I was still an accessory and that would go on my record. Cat had told them that I was just doing him a favor and that I had nothing to do with anything else. The detective released me with a warning. "Young man, let this be a lesson to you. Never allow anyone to use you in that manner no matter friend of foe." "Yes sir, I realized that the request was a little suspect but he was a friend and I trusted him. "Never again." It did prove that CAT was really a friend because he didn't have to expose himself and there would have been nothing that I could have done about it. Cecil A. Turner, C.A.T., I finally knew his name but what a way to find out. He was later convicted of distributing of illegal drugs and served 2 years in the Cook County Jail. If Moms knew what had transpired, it would absolutely kill her and she would kill me. The thing I hated most other than my now having a record was not being able to spend the ten big ones that had been promised by Cat. Under the circumstances, I am fortunate to have my freedom. It was a close call.

Now getting a good job where they would do a thorough background check would be impossible. Walking in and out of places, after being told that they had no opportunities, really made a career in basketball even more appealing. Having people less qualified than I was, tell me that I lack experience just rubbed me the wrong way. Many of these brothers from another mother couldn't recognize talent if it was wrapped around their worthless necks.

Flipping hamburgers and wearing those sissy ass uniforms is not my idea of employment but a brother needs a job and I was ready to do most anything, on the legal side, to earn some dough.

As I walked toward down town with an old broken down fence on my left, I noticed an advertisement for help at Sammy's Car Wash and Auto Repair, hanging precariously on one board. Below the weathered writing was a number to call. Now would come the challenge of finding a phone booth in an area where not only the phone book would usually be missing but sometimes the phone itself. These wine heads around Chicago would try to sell anything to get a bottle of Ripple or some cough syrup. As I turn the corner headed in the direction of the car wash, a booth was across the street at the next corner. I hurried to cross the street and just as I started to step off the curb, a cab nearly ran me over. A voice came from the cab cursing me out in French or German or something.

After finally negotiating the busy avenue, I was lucky to find the phone intact. I dialed the number that was on the poster and a young lady with a sultry voice answered. For the first time I felt that employment was within my reach especially if a woman was to make the decision. "Hello, may I help you", "yes", was the response from the other end. "Yes, my name is August James and I noticed that you had openings at the car wash, is that correct?" "Yes sir we do. What you need to do is come down and fill out an application as soon as possible because there are only a few openings left."

Now how would I get there in time to make this happen? The car wash was 8 blocks away and they were to close in 30 minutes so I had to get on my get-e-up to make it in time. As quick and fast as I was, it would still be a challenge. I made it with about 5 minutes to spare. I entered the front door and walked toward a desk in the far corner of the room. A young red head greeted me with a smile and asked if I was the gentlemen that had called. "Yes, I am August James but all my friends call me AJ and that's what I want you to call me because I feel already that we will be friends so when can I start?"

I have to admit that I was on my game today. There was no way she could recover from that smooth cellophane that I had just wrapped around her. She smiled back not being able to look me in the eyes. I knew then that I was in. "Sir . . . I mean AJ", she said shyly, "have you ever worked in a car wash before?" "I have if you think that would help", I said as I leaned in toward her." "But Sir, I am sorry, I mean . . . AJ, my boss is looking for dependable experienced workers because we have been losing business because of the quality of our service." "What's your name?" I said. "My name is Wanda." "Well, please to meet you Wanda and because time is short and I know you have to close so let's do this. You need workers and I need a job and I am sure you won't be disappointed with the quality of any of my work", I said as I gave her my patented smile and wink. Her next words were, "Ok, ok, I don't know why I am doing this but if anyone ask, you have worked at a car wash before so I won't get in trouble. When can you start?" "I said to her, "I just did." She knew exactly why she was doing it. She wanted some of this vanilla chocolate and she knew it. What she said was music to my ears. Finally I can buy a lady some dinner, put some petro in my ride and save a buck or two. Maybe Ashley can keep her mouth off of a brother for asking for a loan or two. She had really propped the old boy up in his time of need and now maybe I can return the favor.

I couldn't wait to get up the next morning to go to my first gig. I showered did my daily routine and headed for the car wash. I could drive now because now I can put some petro in my tank. I backed out of the garage to Luther Vandross singing "Let's Make Tonight the Night" and I was sailing on cloud nine. As I entered the parking lot, I saw Wanda getting out of a blue Toyota and some guy was trying to kiss her goodbye but she nixed his effort and hurried to the side door of the carwash as he drove away. "Wanda", I called out, it's me, AJ . . . . here live and in living color. I just wanted to thank you for what you did yesterday and I won't let you down I promise." She smiled with a suggestive bite of the bottom lip and responded with, "I hope not, I really hope not." There was more in that second "hope not" than meets the eye. That girl was coming on to me big time and I have to admit, she was not hard on the eyes and had two nice apples following her in that tight dress she was wearing.

The first day was a drag because there was very little traffic through that day but the second day was a different story and they worked my butt off. As I returned home after my day on the job, Chantal met me at the door letting me know that Ashley had called. I picked up the phone to dial Ashley because I had made some nice tips and I could take her out for a night cap and finally follow up on what we should have done at dinner. "Hello Ash, Chantal told me that you had called . . . What's up?" "Oh nothing AJ, just wanted to say how proud I am that you are working and enjoying your new job." "Yes Ash, it feels good to be working though it's only a minimum wage job but it will allow me to save a bit and not mooch off you so much. You know a brother has to contribute something." That's cool AJ, I am just happy that you are happy." "Ash, want to go out for a drink or something?" Thanks AJ, I would love too but I have an early start tomorrow and it's my long day so I am turning in early. Maybe I can come by and have lunch on Friday?" "Yea, that's cool . . . . Ok, sleep well and see you on Friday."

On Friday at Lunch, Ash pulled up in her cream colored Infinity looking fine to the nine. As I greeted her with a slight kiss on the jaw as I got in on the passenger side, I could see Wanda looking through the window as we pulled off. After a nice lunch with Ashley, she dropped me off, giving me a wave as she left. As I headed toward the change room, a voice came from near the office area. "AJ, are you married or was that your girl friend." Oh, what's up Wanda? No that was a friend of mine. We see each other from time to time." "Oh . . . is it the type relationship that would prevent you and me from going out sometimes?" I smiled, "Wanda, I didn't know you wanted to go out with me. What about the dude who drops you off every day?" "I am letting him hang around until I say no. AJ, you tell me yes . . . . I'll tell him no." "We will see Wanda but be careful what you ask for pretty lady." "AJ, whatever you throw . . . . I can catch so you marinate on that for a while, my handsome friend." Wanda was pushing my button and she knew it. We both knew that things had to come to a head sooner or later.

I had decided not to enter the fall semester because the money was not that good but it kept grits and biscuits on the table which was my contribution. I had finally saved enough money to get my own place. Moms wouldn't let Chantal come to live with me because she thought me to be too unstable. She was right if I have to say so myself. I try to spend as much time with Chantal as possible. I was determine that she would be like Reba and attend one of the premiere schools.

The years had hurried by and hanging out with Pookie and Maurice had become my past time. Pookie was my best friend growing up and I had not laid eyes on the sucker during the semester. During my time at school, Pookie would not come around because he felt uncomfortable around the college crowd. Usually he is always under foot but for the last week since classes stopped, I had not heard hide nor hair of that pest of a so called friend. He must have finally found someone who was willing to put up with his trifling butt other than me. He carries around the old beat up mobile phone but either the thing never works or it's strictly for show. It's like people who send flowers to themselves to make people think that someone cares. Pookie is one of those individuals who was dropped on his head at birth and was drop kicked across the room because he is so damn ugly. I don't discriminate against ugly so he is my best friend. Pookie dropped out of kindergarten so he wasn't into the school thing.

I was now well entrenched in a position at Sammy's Car Wash. It was nearing lunch time and I was dead tired from smiling at these honkies and uppity blacks coming through the car wash with their Benzes, BMW's and Cadi's. Many of them just one unfortunate incident away from being right here in this car wash getting dirty and smelling like old soap, just like me.

As the irritating whistle sounded for my one hour lunch break, here comes Pookie, rushing toward me with a panicked look on that ugly face of his. "Man what ails you?" I asked. "Listen AJ, I overheard this dude mentioning your name and he seemed mighty pissed." "Pissed about what? Did you know him Pookie?" Hell no, man, I could not get a good look at him because of his hoodie but what I did see of him, I didn't recognize. All I know is he was a big dude with light skin; the dude could have been white for all I know. Man, he was shouting, cussing and gesturing in a very threatening way. AJ, were you messing with this dud's lady or something?" "Go on Pookie, I hadn't done nothing to nobody. You must have heard it wrong." "AJ, how many people do you know around here named AJ? You better watch your back my trusting and most naive brother.

"Pookie, shut the hell up. Man you need to take something for that diarrhea of the mouth. You been talking since you stumbled your raggedy ass in here now do you want something to eat or what? You are wasting my time." "All right mista know nothing . . . . " Pookie, it's "KNOW IT ALL", not "know nothing". Man you are a trip." Pookie and I went over to a little greasy spoon restaurant just across Main Street to get a sandwich and cup of coffee. I knew he would show up around lunch time to get a free meal. Though I didn't let Pookie know it but my mind began to wonder about who it was asking about me. I have never had issue with anyone other than a small riff with a dude in jail when I was convicted of shop lifting 3 years back. I had to whip a dude's tail because he was trying to bitch me out. He threatened to get even with me when he got out but I heard that he was canceled by a 357 magnum in the hands of his old lady for abusing her. Other than that incident, old AJ has kept his nose clean. There was the Shawn ordeal but that white boy didn't want any more of me. He was a little embarrassed that I was able to trump him with that fine Faye. That's been several years ago so I know that dude is over that by now. I see him around town with a fine, big legged white girl so he must have gotten over Faye.

She has to be special because forgetting Faye ain't easy. Maybe he finally realized that he was out of his league.

As the months hurried by, I had yet to decide to finish my last year at Northwestern. I had gotten into a little trouble selling drugs trying to make ends meet a few years back and that shit was on my record now. A stupid mistake like that will unfortunately follow me for the rest of my life. Luckily, I was given a short sentence because of my past good record and only had to spend a few months in the joint and was allowed to walk because of good behavior.

The money at the car wash was weak but it kept the old boy in sneakers and gas in my car. I was able to put aside ten percent from my pay check plus tips had given me enough to rent an apartment. Four years had gone by and I was still washing cars and putting a few dollars away for emergencies but more importantly, had not finished my last year at Northwestern.

Just as I took the last bite of the heart attack burger, the phone rang. I had to clean my hands because of the mustard, catsup and grease that poured from the waxed paper that was used to keep the paper bag from getting soaked. Viewing the screen and not recognizing the number, I decided to let it go into voice mail. It was a long distance call and my bill was high enough as it was. A few minutes later, the phone rang again. Now who could want me that bad to keep calling me like this? As I picked up the phone, a familiar voice said," AJ, it's me, Reba, don't you remember. "Oh yes, yes Reba, how are you?" Now I'm stuck." It's been a long time girl; I thought that you had forgotten us poor folks back here in Chicago. "AJ, why haven't I heard from you, you said that you would keep in touch?" Well Reba, I got busy and you know that a brother has to make a living." "So tell me AJ, what are you doing these days?

You didn't even think to invite me to graduation." "Well Reba, I did not get around to graduating yet and life came in conflict with my finishing school but I still plan to though." Reba was an extraordinary person but I had blown the relationship during my pot smoking, macking days back at Northwestern. She was my perfect dream of a woman back then and I had let her slip right through my fingers. Man, she had a body that had perfection written all over it and legs that Tina Turner would be jealous of. She was never one to chase after guys because the girl was focused on her future for which I was not to be a part of. One thing about Reba is that she is no non-sense and she didn't play. When she got wind of my smoking that funny weed, she made it clear that we were headed in different directions and dropped me like a Mohammed Ali right cross.

As I took my hand from over the phone to acknowledge her, I realized that she had been right all the time. She had told me that I wouldn't amount to nothing because of my habits and "nothing" was what I had become. I cleared my throat and spoke again, "Reba, where are you?" "I am in Indianapolis for a legal conference and you crossed my mind. I will be here for a few days if you want to get together for a few drinks and catch up. It's only a short ride from Chicago." "Yea, Reba . . . I know but it's a bad time for me. My Pops has been ill and I have to stay close in case he or Moms need something. With Moms working and everything, I have to stay close." I was lying my ass off but what else can I do, I couldn't let her know what a looser I had become.

I really wanted to see Reba and wrap my arms around those great curves of hers but I knew better. How could I face her with my life being in the shambles that it is? How did she look after four years and was she giving that nectar to any of those Ivy League guys. "Reba, I am trying to close up now but can I call you later to let you know? "AJ, don't play with me now, I look for you to keep your promise and call me back." "I will Reba, I promise." I closed the lid on my cell phone, I breathed a brief sigh of relief because I dodged a bullet on that one, but what do I do now? Do I call her back or not?

"AJ, you been sitting here and fat mouthing with everyone as if I wasn't here. Who the hell is Reba anyway", said Pookie. "Don't remember you talking about her, you been holding out on old Pookie."

"Man, that was one that I let slip through my fingers back during my last semester in college. She is Indy and wants me to come over to see her while she is there. "You going, said Pookie?" "Hell to the no man! You must be tripping. Reba was well out of my league then and now and I would be embarrassed to just hold a conversation with her. What would I say . . . . Oh by the way Reba, I work in a car wash, notwithstanding the fact that Ashley would murderize a brother? Ashley has been too good to me to screw up. Reba can tempt the most honest brother with what she has. She is gorgeous and brainy." "You better believe it AJ, you think that the guy that was cussing you out is a problem, man Ashley is nice but she is a street chick and she will tear your family jewels out and feed them to you one at a time and you know that I'm right. Also, I would tell her." "Tell her what? Pookie are you out of your crazy ass mind?" "That's right AJ, I will sing like a bird in a window on Sunday morning", said Pookie. "Pookie, don't play, I got enough trouble as it is and I definitely don't need your ass screwing things up more for me."

I wolfed down part of the sandwich and quickly hurried back to finish my shift leaving Pookie sucking down French fries like a vacuum cleaner. I couldn't wait until 5:00 pm. to get away from this hell hole. As I washed my last car of the evening, a 2008 Lexus, I noticed a car parked across the street from the car wash. As I stood gazing at the late model red Ford Mustang with 22's, the driver slowly pulled off and seemed to point in my direction. It was probably nothing but my imagination playing tricks on me. I remembered that Shawn had pointed at me and Faye in that same manner but that dude couldn't be holding a grudge that long, or could he? Off in the distance, it did seem like a white boy.

Finally the hour was at hand and I quickly dried my hands, placed my equipment in the locker, and carefully slid my size 12 feet out of the boots so that my socks would stay on. They were a little soggy from standing in water all day. I tried to hurry to the time clock before there was a line. I knew that I had to speed it up because the Mid

Town bus waits for no mother's son. I finally arrived at the bus stop with about five minutes to spare. The driver was beginning to close the doors when he heard me banging on the back door. I stepped on to the bus with a sigh of relief because I definitely didn't want to be stranded on that side of town waiting 30 minutes for the next bus. It would eat into my little stash of money to have to grab a cab so I was pleased that the driver had it in his heart to open the door.

I remembered that Reba was expecting a call and as much as I wanted to see her, I knew that it was impossible and I can't lie to Reba, she could see right through me. I will put off calling her until later when I get home. As I boarded the Mid Town bus headed home after an evening of washing cars for people who didn't even know I existed, I decided to set in a seat nearest to the back door so that I could have a good view of the folks getting on an off the bus.

It was 6:00 pm now and riding the mid town bus was akin to getting combat pay for serving in Vietnam. Every slimy creature that had crawled from underneath every rock in the city seemed to find their way to this mid town bus route. As I set dreading even going home to the dreary apartment, I slowly slid my hand into my pocket to see how I had done with the evening tips from busting my behind washing cars for people who literally hate me not only because I was black but because I was not at their socio-economic level. A quarter fell to the floor and rolled about 2 feet and rested under a seat across the aisle. Damn, I can't afford to lose a dime so I tucked the rest back in my pocket and moved quickly to rescue my quarter. Once back in my seat I carefully removed the change again without dropping anything this time. To my surprise I had been blessed with tips totaling $95.35. It was my best day ever at the car wash. The people who get their car's washed at Sammy's were pretty good tippers. I was nothing for them to drop a ten on a brother so sometimes I did more in tips than in my pay check.

The $95 will come in handy until I get my check on Friday. In fact it's about as much as I get in my regular check anyway. It's almost embarrassing to admit that I am settling for a minimum wage job but it is what it is. I am sure that Reba would be proud of me. Yea, right!!! A man gotta do what a man gotta do to get along in this ghetto of a world. Why do I put up with this meager existence when there are better options out there for me?

I had blown every opportunity to make something out of myself by dropping out of school and now I am washing cars for a lousy living with no end in sight. I knew the importance of an education but I had no one constantly reminding me so I took the easy way out. I was good at basketball, baseball and track but the pull of the streets was stronger than any of my God given talents. How can I motivate myself to go back to school when there are degreed people working with me at the car wash because of the lack of jobs in Chicago? The little hope that I had to eventually get out of this rat hole was being challenged by reality as life play these war games with me.

As my bus crossed Pine Avenue, I could see that this was not going to be a pleasant evening. A soft mist had started to cover the streets, which normally is a sure indicator in the Windy City that the worst weather was yet to come. The wind had started to move the bus from side to side, and sheets of paper and trash could be seen flying by the window. As we passed vacant lots, these miniature tornadoes could be seen stirring up more of the trash and garbage lying in the cutters and on the sidewalks. This was reminiscent of the dust storms I remember seeing rumbling across the dusty roads at grandma house down in New Orleans when I was a kid. Sometimes I wish I could go back to that time when there were no worries, few responsibilities and always plenty to eat on the table. That seems now to be so long ago.

At that instant, the phone rang again and I knew it was Reba. I didn't even bother to look at the screen nor did I answer it. As my conscious tugged at me, I decided to return the call to Reba and face the music. But as I gazed down at the phone screen, I realized that it was Ashley who had called and not Reba. Before I call Ashley, I decided to call Reba and tell her that I would meet her for a drink on Friday. I dialed the number still unsure of what I would say. The phone rang at least 7 times and just as I had decided to hang up, Reba picked up. "Hello, is that you AJ? There was a silent pause on my part because fear was creeping in slowly but surely. "AJ, is that you?" "Oh, yes, yes Reba, it's me, how are you?" "Thanks for calling me back. I really wanted to hear from you. Now make me very happy by telling me that you are on your way to Indy, please, please." "Well Reba, I do want to see you and catch up so what about Friday. I will try to get there around 8:00 pm, does that work?" "Anytime you get here works for me." Now I am cautious but carrying a grin from ear to ear because she was excited to see old AJ. Maybe, a little of the attraction that was always there between Reba and me still had a little of its magic.

I was beginning to warm up to the idea because of the excitement in her voice. I was on cloud nine but unknowingly, the cloud was about to burst and deliver a downpour that would have me water logged. "OK Reba, I will see you Friday." As I hung up from Reba feeling good about myself, I quickly phoned Ashley to let her know that I would be at my flat soon and would call her. Ashley picked up on the first ring. AJ, why haven't I heard from you all day?" "Ah Ash, give a brother a break, it's been a long day and I did pretty good on my tips today. Maybe we can go out and get some barbeque later." "I don't want to go anywhere in this weather. What I was calling about was my wing at the hospital is having a roast for one of the doctors who is leaving and I really want you to go with me. It's important to me AJ because he has been really supportive of me and has helped me tremendously over the years." When is it Ash? "It's this Friday at the Ritz Carlton and you know I love that place. You can spring for a massage if you want too." "Girl, now you are really tripping, where the hell will I get enough money to pay for a massage at that place? You sure it is this Friday?" "Yes, it is this Friday. Do you have something better to do? You never take me anywhere so I hope you are not even thinking about trying to get out of it."

My stomach started to do flips. How did I get myself into this mess? Of all times for her to go out with those stuff shirts that she work with, she had to pick the same day that I had committed to Reba to meet her in Indy. "Ash, Ash, Ash" . . . . I pretended to have a bad connection and hung up so I would have time to think. It was either my Girl or my Dream girl. What a mess I had gotten myself into. My day had gone from bad to tsunami.

Ashley was my girl, for now. She and I had been dating on an off for the past few years and she picked me up after the unfortunate run in with the law. She did not judge me and always encouraged me to improve myself. She was a Nurse's Aide at Mercy Hospital and Medical Center across town. She is a smart, dedicated street girl but did have a lot of class about her and a temper something fierce. When she got angry, it lasted for a long time which affected my love life and the ability to knock the hell out of those boots, if you get my drift. Her family always thought that I was no good for her but I had worked hard to get into their favor. Now when they find out about this, and she will tell them, I will be right back at square one. *(I don't know what it is about us men but we tend to take adventure and living on the edge more serious than making common sense decisions)*

The bus driver stopped to let a few passengers off and a few on at each stop along the route. The night seemed uneventful so far and that was completely fine with me. The normal cast of Neanderthals must have been aware of the approaching weather and had opted to stay in their caves. As the bus approached 15th and Madison, the wind started to swirl harder and harder, when suddenly I could hear the huge rain drops bouncing off the top of the bus. The drops were so large that it sounded like it was hailing. The sky opened up and poured rain in buckets, it seemed, and lightning seemed to strike the buildings just up ahead of us. Why couldn't God have just waited a few more minutes to give me a chance to get home? The gall of me to even think that I can question God's work! One thing that all ways stuck with me was my grandmother telling us to unplug all of the electrical stuff in the house like the toaster, the TV and the stereo and sit quietly while the almighty does his work.

The bus rocked and swerved in the down pour as sheets of water scattered people on the sidewalks as the bus passed. The bus finally arrived at my stop and as I stepped off, I couldn't help but get the eerie feeling that I was being watched. It was only a passing feeling though because no one cared about AJ and I had no grudge with anybody. I did still owe a debt from my days of smoking that funny weed but the dealer that I was working with had long been jailed for money laundering and possession of over a quarter of a million dollars in cocaine. That "White Horse" has been the death of many a dealer and their users. I didn't want that to be my fait so I decided to clean up my act. I wonder if that old debt is coming back to haunt me. I surely hope not because I have been clean and have no desire to return to smoking that devil weed ever again. It still sometimes calls my name but believe me, I ain't listening no more.

The bus stop was approximately 3 blocks from my flat so I had to make a mad dash toward home before I was totally water logged. I took off all my jewelry before leaving the bus to keep the lightning from striking me. As I ran for home, the water splashing from my shoes hitting the sidewalk was so intense that it had started to fill my Kmart special sneakers. My running and the wet shoes made it sound as if I had rubber galoshes on. I finally reached the porch which had a small stoop over it to shield the front door from the devastating summer sun. Here in Chicago, very little can shield a person from the cold and heartless winters that causes every bone in your body to ache like a terrible case of pneumonia.

As I stood under the stoop fumbling for my door keys, that feeling hit me again. It was stronger than ever this time. Why was I feeling as if I was being watched? I turned and did a quick scan of the immediate area but everything seemed ok with the exception of the weather taking a turn for the worse. Finally getting the key in the door and pushing to get inside gave me some relief but I was soaked from head to toe. As I climbed the inner stairs to my front door, I could hear my stomach growling after only eating that grease burger and fries for lunch. The though hit me that it would have been great getting home to a cozy house and a warm meal but quickly I pinched myself and woke up from that dream. I use to go to Mama's house after work to get a meal but Mama had not fixed a meal since she started to ride the white horse. As for my Pops, he is so wasted by the time he gets home that food is the farthest thing from his pickled mind. My hunger pains would continue until the weather lets up and I was able to go down the street to McDonalds or convince Ashley to go with me for barbeque.

As I stepped into the flat, it gave me little comfort from the feeling that had come over me. I immediately took off my sneakers and poured the water into a bucket that was near the door. I took off my socks and clothes and put on my bath robe. I took a few deep breaths lit a cigarette and strolled to the window to see who else had fallen victim to the elements as I had. While near the window, I checked the messages on the house phone. The first one that came up was Ashley asking me to call as soon as I get in the door. I could tell by the tone of her voice that she was not happy that I had not answered her question and had not finished the conversation. I picked up the phone to call her without knowing what to say. I was playing Russian roulette with my life, my relationship with Ashley but nothing would keep me from something that I had dreamed about ever since she left. I desperately wanted to see Reba and rekindle, if only for a moment, what we had before.

The phone started to ring and immediately Ash picked up. "AJ, what took you so long to call me and why did you hang up on me?" "Girl, quit tripping, we had a bad connection and I didn't try to call back because the weather was getting worse and I wanted to wait until I got home. I am calling you now right, so slow your roll"! "What's this attitude I am hearing from you AJ? Do I detect an attitude?" "Nah Ash, but, but . . . . . " "But what AJ?" "Ash, I can't go to the Ritz with you on Friday cause I have to go to Indy to see an old buddy of mine. I had committed to him that I would visit when he passed through and he is coming in on Friday. That's what I was trying to tell you when we were talking before but we were cut off." "Why you never told me about this before now with your trifling ass and what buddy are you lying about. I know you didn't just plan this today AJ. If you didn't want to go to the event with me why didn't you just man up and say it? Don't play me AJ, I don't ask you for much but this is important to me." "Come on Ash, you remember Raymond Renolds who went off to play with the San Francisco 49ers. We called him RAY when he was back on the block. I told you about him many times. That was a bad dude with the pig skin. He had been trying to get up with me every time he came through and I was always tied up." "AJ, YOU ARE TIED UP AGAIN AND I AM NOT TAKING NO FOR AN ANSWER. If you do not go with me to this . . . . you will regret it my lying brother and don't think for a minute that I am buying that Ray Ray shit. Whoever you are going to see, I hope it's worth it because it could cost you a lot."

"That's the Perry Mason shit coming out in Ash right now", I said to myself. It's like she reads my thoughts. I didn't want to lose her but I wasn't going to give up an opportunity to see Reba again. The old conscious was whipping my tail. The good devil on the right said," AJ, stay your tail in Chicago and take Ash to the Ritz and the bad devil on the left shoulder said, Man, this may be your last chance to tap Reba and hold those curves in the palm of your hands just one more time. Needless to say, the devil on the left shoulder won. Ash had been mad with me before and got over it so what's different this time. I still didn't feel good about it. "Ash, would I do you like that, I wouldn't do it if I had not cancelled all the other hookups we tried to have. The brother is cool and I hoped you would understand." Just then my ears were ringing from the sound of the phone hanging up on Ash's end. She was thoroughly pissed and I was feeling like shit because I had lied to her again.

Reba was in Indy and ready to rekindle our old friendship and I was heading into the perfect storm. I got up early Friday morning headed to work knowing that the evening was hopefully going to be one to remember. I couldn't help but wonder what Ash would do about the Ritz; she had gone to events before without me. I had never experienced the anger like last night. The day seemed to drag by in anticipation of seeing Reba. Even the attitudes of the snobs and silver spooners did not affect me today. Nothing was going to ruin my mood . . . . I thought.

Just a few blocks away, Shawn and Portia, a tall and well stacked tenderoni, were having a serious conversation. "Portia, what's up girl, I see you haven't lost any of the spark that made you homecoming queen a few years ago." "Shawn, I am always going to keep all of this in the right place, if you know what I mean. It's a mean world out there and these Chicago women are trying to get their hooks in any man who can walk upright. As for me, there must be something special about any man who rubs up against all of this and that special thing is a job and plenty of money. These trifling ass men here in Chicago want you to take care of them. Well they have the wrong tree to bark up because they get nothing here." "Portia, Portia . . . . something never change. You still have as much piss and vinegar as you ever had." "So Shawn, to what do I owe this chance encounter. Knowing you, there is something up your sleeve other than those muscular arms." "Since you put it that way, I do have a favor to ask and if you do it, we can spend a little time together just like old times and I am sure that I can make you smile like I did back in the day." "White Boy please, the only reason I was smiling back then is because you spend the money on a girl and my black solders didn't have even a closed bank account. Most of them couldn't help me if they wanted too. As far as your love making Shawn, I hope you have gotten more practice since then, my less than Nubian brother. By the way, weren't you and that hustler Faye an Item? Don't tell me she kicked you to the curb." "Girl, stop trippin, you don't give a bro a break for nothing. I did the kicking but that's another story. This dude was undercutting me with Faye and embarrassed me in front of my boys and he has to pay. No one threatens me with a weapon and lives to enjoy it."

"So Shawn, what has that got to do with me? With your reputation of leaving bodies all over Chicago, what makes this one different?" "Look Portia, we have been friends for a long time so do this one thing for me and you can call your prize as long as it not a car or something crazy expensive." "Shawn, you are serious. Who is this masked man and what do you want me to do with him?" "Portia, I just want to you attract this dude to your nectar and that should be easy as fine as wine as you are. He will take the bait because this guy thinks he is the God's gift to women and will screw a snake if you hold the head. When he gets an eye full of your fine ass, he will flip out and do some crazy shit which will fall right into my hands. I want you to get him to come to your apartment and I will be waiting for his sorry ass with more than a big stick." Wait-a-minute, don't be planning nothing in my apartment that will have the cops looking for me. Whatever you are planning had better be prior to his getting to my place am I making myself clear? Shawn, I like you white boy, but this shit I am not sure about. Who is this guy that's making your brain pregnant anyway?" His name is AJ and he works at the car wash down the street. That sucker was tipping with Faye behind my back and no one does me that way, . . . no one." "Shawn, it sounds to me like you are after the wrong person. He couldn't do anything that she didn't let him do." "Don't worry, her time comes next and it won't be pretty."

"Ok, back to what's in it for me. I saw this mesmerizing fur jacket that cost six thousand dollars down at Gino's Furs, that is out of my range but I want it so bad. That's what I want, nothing more, nothing less. If I attract this AJ to my place, just make sure that I am not tied to your ass in any way. I don't want this brother coming after me like you are doing to him." "Believe me Portia, he want be able to follow anyone when I am finished with his ugly ass." "Ok, I will try my best and don't play with me Shawn, I want my coat and I may give you a little "some um" "some um" to remember me by if you can handle it", Portia said as she slowly spread her legs tightening her well fitted dress to accent every curve in her gorgeous body. "So, how do I identify this AJ person anyway?" You will know him because he is the only high yellow black dude on the wash line. He refuses to wear the company overalls so he will be the guy in the white smock." "He is there for another couple of hours if you can get over there today Portia." What's the rush Shawn, can't you give a girl a chance to get use to the idea and plan my "gotcha game?" "Portia, your "gotcha" game is always in high gear so please go over there before he gets off, please. I am well overdue in paying this clown back for what he did." "Ok, Shawn, I am on my way now but I hope this guy is as easy as you seem to think." Portia walked toward her car with Shawn staring as the motion of her ocean. "Shawn, quit looking at my behind, it will cause you to be cross eyed my anxious friend."

As Portia pulled into line at the car wash, many of the men were straining to get a look at who was driving the Beamer. As Portia approached being next in line, she slowly got out of the car with as much leg showing as possible without exposing the obvious gold mind hidden beneath. She had on a short, sequenced, tighter than hell, dress with all things matching to the nine. Even while looking like a million dollars, that fine tenderoni, in her Pearl White BMW 300 series did not sway me from my appointed rounds with Reba. Any other time, there would be no way that I wouldn't get those digits and add them to my player portfolio.

I know that I am a bad dude but there was something wrong with this picture. She did everything but come over and un-dress in front of me, trying to get my attention. The girl was stacked, not hard to look at, with a booty like Faye's. It was obvious that she was well taken care of because of the diamonds on her hand and in her ears. I walked over to her and asked what particular service did she want? Her response was, "full service, for my car and . . . me." This girl was too obvious. I had met forward women before but for one who didn't know me from Adams house cat, she was somewhat suspect. I didn't take the bait. I reached for her keys and found myself in a tug of war. She was staring deeply into my eyes but held tightly to the keys. "Will I get my request or not?" I gave her an emphatic, "yes I will take care of your car" and snatched the keys from her hand. A girl as well kept as her seemed a bit out of place trying for a pick up at the car wash. This woman could call her shots at the best places in Chicago so what was this all about? Old AJ didn't just fall off the cabbage truck. This felt like a set up. I kept my eyes on her while the car was being taken care of and she did the same to me. I could feel her presence as I went about my duties.

When the car was wiped clean and sparkling like new money, I walked up to the hold area to let her know that the car was finished. She was busy talking on the cell phone. As I approached her, she walked out of range so that I couldn't hear her conversation. "Shawn, this guy is either gay or he is a cold fish. I have never had a man not ask for my number when I all but offered him the works. What do you want me to do?" "Try sliding him your number and see if he takes it. If he takes it, he has fallen for the bait. If he doesn't, we are back at square one." As she walked back toward me, she took a card from her purse. "Ms. ah, ah . . . I didn't catch your name." "That's because I didn't give it. Who is asking anyway?" "Without any sign of being friendly, I said, "My name is AJ and I just wanted to tell you that your car is ready." "Well that's more like it Mr. AJ and my name is Portia and it's indeed a pleasure to meet you. What about the second part of my request?" "Thanks but no thanks, though I am flattered, I have to get back to work Portia and it was nice meeting you too." "AJ, can't you give a girl a call sometimes, I usually don't have to work this hard to get someone to call me." She reached out and grabbed my hand and placed her card in my palm. "I am not in the habit of giving out my number to anyone who has no intention of using it. Will you use it?" I smiled and backed away leaving Portia to wonder if I would or not. If she was on the up and up, I had the upper hand and I would play it only if I chose to do so. I walked a few feet away and decided to look back. If she was still standing there looking disgusted, I had played the right card but if she had turned to walk away, this had been more than just a visit to the car wash. I turn and Portia was still standing there looking as pissed as ever. A fine woman like that, it had to hurt to be given the brush off as I did to her. Though I felt good by her reaction and I probably would follow up with a call, I still couldn't get it out of my heads that this was too easy. All of a sudden, I am being surrounded with opportunity and beautiful women.

Portia immediately got on the phone to Shawn to tell him how things went. "Shawn, what the hell did you do to me? Man that guy is no push over. He all but made me feel like a hooker trying to run a game. I did everything but screw him on the spot and that cold fish threw water on my fire." "Well Portia, thanks for trying and usually there is more than one way to skin a cat. If I can't get to him one way, I will find another. He has a fine little baby sister that is ready to be plucked." "Wait, just hold on Shawn. I know you are not talking about what I think you are talking about. That's sick so keep me out of any more of your devious plans. I am out of here."

Chapter VIII

Reba's Return

After work, I hurried home and put on my hounds tooth jacket, black pants and my black gators. I snapped on my kangoe, placed an extra amount of love portion on my neck and the chest hair that was slightly showing above the unbuttoned silk black shirt. Man I was so sharp that I cut myself three times before I got out of the flat. As I started to open the door on my way out, the phone rang again. "Now what", I said to myself. Could it be Ashley taking one final shot at me or was it Reba making sure I was still coming. I thought it best that I not take a chance and have to do more lying to cover my tracks. As I glanced down at the phone screen, I noticed it was from the hospital and I knew without a doubt that it was Ashley.

My car was in the Garage out back. I did not drive it to work most of the time because it was cheaper to take the bus and I was pinching the hell out of pennies to make ends meet. My ride was a 1994 Mustang, not something a player like me would have but dependable none the less. It was red convertible with a sun roof, saddle interior and a sound system to die for. If Reba did happen to want a ride I was ready. I wasn't worried because I was just going there for a drink or two or three. I licked my fingers, ran them across the front of my cap, slid in the ride and off I went.

As I got about three miles outside the city limits, the phone rang thinking it was Reba checking on my arrival time, I said, "what, you can't wait to see old AJ,?" The voice on the other end said, "AJ, who are you saying that too? Did you change your mind? Are you on your way to get me?" "Shit, its Ashley . . . . now what am I going to do?" I had to think fast, "Hi baby, just kidding, I knew it was you but I was just playing." I am on my way to meet Ray Ray and will be back later tonight. Have a good time at the event." I waited a minute to see if I had dodged the bullet. Not only did I not dodge the thing, it hit me square in the heart. "AJ, I told you not to play with me." Just as quickly as the words left her lips she hung up. A few minutes later, the phone rang again and it was a hospital number but not Ashley's number. Was it Ashley again or someone else? I ignored the call this time and focused on Reba and what I hoped to be a great evening. If the call was important, they would leave a message and I could get it later.

Each white stripe in the highway seemed to slow down almost in slow motion as I wondered what Ashley meant in her comments. As I entered the city of Indy, and made my way to the Marriott Hotel where Reba was staying, I couldn't help but notice the Benz's, BMW'S, Aston Martin's, and Jags coming in and out of the entry. I pulled up to the entry and a bellman asked me if he could help me. Most of the time, they will ask you are you checking in. I guess that was the first sign that I didn't belong. As I entered the lobby, a major hesitation engulfed me as I stood among the who's who of the blue blood society. I had called Reba to let her know that I was in the lobby but that was 10 minutes ago. I stared at my watch for a minute before looking up and seeing Reba coming toward me. She had a sleek black dress that hugged her curves like a silk pillow cases. She was accented with a string of black pearls that cost more than my car, my flat and all of my other possessions two times over. I was certainly out of my league. I was so focused on the majestic figure coming in my direction and didn't notice the 6'4" framed superman just behind her.

"AJ, it's so good to finally see you again, you look good as usual. I want you to meet a good friend of mine Roger, who accompanied me to the event tonight. Roger is one of the partners at the law firm that I work for." At that point my eyes looked like the red and white rotating cylinders outside of most barber shops. Roger reached and grabbed my hand and placed it in a vice like grip that almost caused me to scream out like a little bitch. "Please to meet you Roger, I spurted out. "Likewise I am sure AJ." Roger finally released the torque of a grip on my hand and turned to Reba and said that he would let us visit and that he would be in the ball room. He kissed her on the jaw and did a military turn and was gone. I was still staring at the hunk of a man I have to admit. "AJ, AJ . . . . Are you all right? It's really good to see you my old friend. I am so happy that you came. Are you happy to see me?" "Well yes, Reba, just a little dazed at how lovely you are. You know that you and old AJ are connected girl." "Thanks AJ, let's go into the lounge and catch up." She reached over and kissed me on the cheek and her breast rubbed my arm. It felt like a cloud. They were so soft that she must have sprinkled meat tenderizer or something on them every day for the last month.

Reba, order a bottle of Borolo wine and ask if it was ok if we sit in a corner that had some privacy. I am not the classic wine drinker but I was sharp enough to know that Borolo was top of the line. But what else could I expect, Boonesfarm? I noticed that she pulled up very close to me as if she knew that I was nervous and she would have a calming effect on my nervous ass. Whatever she was trying to do, it was working. "So tell me Reba, what brings you to Nap Town?" "Well AJ, I am here to a conference of lawyers to discuss tort reform." Tort who, I thought? I didn't want her to know that I didn't know what the heck she was talking about. I think she knew it too because she had this sort of sly grin as if to say, I won't embarrass him and believe me, I appreciated it.

"Tell me AJ, what's going on in your life. It's been awhile? Are you seeing anyone?" "Well no, not really. I go out from time to time but nothing serious. What about you Reba?" "Roger and I hang out but I am not ready for the serious stuff, my practice comes first. Roger is cool and secure and have no hang ups about what I do." "Cool, Reba, he seems like a nice guy." "I often think about you and wonder how you are doing. I see now that you are doing just fine", as I gave her one of my patented smiles. "AJ, I have to admit that I think of you also. We had a good friendship once until your habits got in the way." "No one knows that better than me Reba and I still kick myself for that." "Well, that's water over the damn AJ, looking back is only for losers." Just as things were getting interesting, the phone rang again from the same number at the hospital. "AJ, shouldn't you take it, it could be important." "Nah, Reba, if it's important, they will leave a message. Now where were we before the interruption?"

"I am getting a little tipsy AJ, would you walk me to my room to freshen up a bit." It was the first time that I had ever been afraid of a woman but that first time had come" She seemed so in control and I felt out of place. As we got on the elevator, she grabbed my arm and pulled in close to me. I was hoping that she could not hear my heart beating like it was coming out of my chest. As we arrived at the 18 th floor, she guided me to a corroder labeled Master suites. We stop in front of 1823 and she handed me the key and asked that I open the door for her. Once inside, the room opened up into a large living area with couches and chairs that were fit for a king. Reba was definitely a queen and deserved every inch of this glorious pad. I could see that there was a Jacuzzi bath and a shower with a head at each end of the shower stall, probably to accommodate Roger and her. Was this the same Reba that left Chicago? The innocence was definitely gone and she had left the Mormon look far behind and I was enjoying every bit of it.

As I continued to look up an around as if I was standing in time square in New York, Reba appeared with nothing on but a g-string and a bra and 2 glassed for the Champagne that she had chilling in the bed room. My heart was at cardiac arrest stage now but I was just going to have to die because I was going with the flow. All I could think of other that the voluptuous melons hanging off her chest was what if Roger would come in and see us and man I would not stand a chance with that dude. He looked as if he could tackle Mike Tyson with ease.

Reba, sensing my hesitancy, came over to me and gently rubbed my member until it ached like a freshly pulled tooth. She put her tongue in my ear and I was about to explode. She went to a switch on the wall and with a flick, the lights dimmed and soft music from Luther Vandross filled all the empty space in the room with a house is not a home. She had me and she knew it. I was just a pawn on her chest board and she was making the moves and there was nothing I could or wanted to do about it. Before I knew it we were intertwined like a well woven rope. I have never been to heaven but this must be somewhere near it because I was seeing streets of gold and could have sworn that I saw angels.

Reba moaned so loud as she took my member and did thing with it that would have caused Jerry Springer to turn a bright shade of red. She controlled the process like I was her bitch. Sweat was popping off my forehead like the raindrops that was pounding the windows from the storm that still raged outside. The friction from our rotating bodies gave off so much heat that I thought that the sprinklers would go off. It was hard hearing her sensuous moaning over mine. It seemed like only seconds had past but actually it had been close to 45 minutes. As we lay there quiet, I couldn't help but ask. "Reba, what about Roger?" 'What about Roger she shot back? "Well, I thought . . . ", "You think too much AJ" and once again started to thrust and shake on my member until she sucked me completely dry. I had never felt the loss of control as I had at that moment. We both ended up at the foot of the bed somehow but who cared. I was in Reba heaven. Though she was not quite as skilled as Faye, she had the total package. Faye seemed overwhelmed by the lovemaking experience but Reba seemed melancholy. It was if it was just another roll in the hay for her. The Reba that I knew back in college was long gone, you can believe that.

We were laying there in the moment smelling the soft aroma of some serious love making when I must have dozed off. I was awakened by the sounds of the streets below and the voice of other hotel guest moving in the halls. I glanced over Reba to the radio clock on the night stand and it said 6:00am. I popped up hoping that I was mistaken but it was indeed the next morning and though I had the best time of my entire life but that life was in jeopardy when I returned to Chicago.

Reba heard my movement and turn to see me pacing the floor near the window. "What's up AJ? You seem restless." "Nah Reba, I just was supposed to get back last night because I had promised a friend that I would come by and help him move into his new crib." "AJ, some things never change. You couldn't lie well when we were together back in school and you still don't." You are dating someone and now you don't have an excuse for being away all night." "Nah, Reba, you got it wrong, there is no one I have to answer too, you are trippin." Reba started to smile as if to say, yea, right, and turned back over. "By the way, what happened to Roger . . . . was he not staying here with you?" "You let me worry about Roger. Unlike you, I have my life in order and Roger knows what time it is."

Boy, I must be a cheap novel because these chicks are reading me chapter and verse. "Yo Reba, I gotta go now but when can I see you again?" "Why do you want to see me again AJ, it seems that very little has changed since I last saw you. You are still not in control of your life." "Listen Girl, last night was the bomb and I want to see you again and soon." "No AJ, it was just sex, good sex I have to admit, but just sex. We both enjoyed the moment so let's move on. Not once during our love making did you say how you felt about me. I was really waiting for that. Please lock the door on the way out. Good seeing you again AJ."

I had just had a lesson in total control and my teacher had just burst my bubble. I thought that I had just completed the master piece of my career in love making and it was reduced to a one night stand by the finest instructor this side of Chicago. I had just been raped by the master rapist and still had to face Ashley. Ashley was no slouch in bed but she was an amateur compared to Reba and Faye. I set in my car for what seemed like hours just taking in what just happened. I knew that it would probably be the last time I would see Reba but I could say that both Faye and Reba were in a class of their own. I headed back to Chi Town hoping that the ride back would give me some ideas of how to face Ash.

The storm had passed over now and things seemed calm but what was in store for me when I get back to Chicago. It was a long ride back thinking of how to smooth this over with Ashley. The mind is a terrible thing to waste and my mind was spilling all over the car seat. I had no idea what to say to Ashley about my meeting with Ray Ray. How could I have chosen seeing an old friend over taking Ash to this event that was important to her? She was the one always in my corner but also always the one at the bottom of my list. I kept stepping into a pile of cow dong and didn't have the sense to clean my shoes off.

I parked in the garage and sundered up to the apartment. I usually get a call from Ashley on Saturday morning so I checked the messages. The only message that I had was from Pookie. His message was that he had some important information for me. Pookie never calls me so what was it now? I picked up the phone to dial. "Pookie, what's up dude?" "AJ, man you better cover your tail. I saw that same car that was at the car wash cruising the neighborhood today. It passed your crib at least three times man so you better watch your back."

Now I am really trippin because this is too much of a coincidence. Why was this same car showing up at the car wash and now on my street? I had a lot on my mind and wasn't thinking clearly. "Ok Pookie, good looking out. I don't know who would think I was important enough to worry about but something is up. Thanks again for looking out for a brother but I am sure it's just a coincidence.

Man I have been screwing up royally lately. I went to Indianapolis to see Reba, my old flame and I didn't take Ash to an event at the hospital. I need to call her to smooth things over." "Alright my male whore of a friend. These women are going to rip your balls off and feed them to you one at a time." "Ha, ha my brother, I got this. Ash will come around, you will see."

As I hung up the phone, there was still no call from Ash. What was up with her? She had always been so predictable. I would have normally heard from her by now. Now it was getting late in the day and still no call. Against my better judgment, I picked up the phone to call her but there was no answer. I tried her cell phone but with the same result. It was not like Ashley to not return my calls so something wasn't right.

As I took off my clothes to relax a bit, I had forgotten to turn my phone back on. On the screen was another call from the hospital. As I opened my voice mail, my mother's voice was the first I heard." AJ, where are you? Please, please call us as soon as possible. Chantal is in the hospital and is in critical condition. She was attacked on the way home from school. That's all I can say right now but please call." My heart seemed to jump right out of my chest. I couldn't believe what I had just heard. Was I dreaming? When the initial shock wore off, I hurried to dress and headed for the hospital. Why couldn't I have answered the calls? While I was out chasing dreams with Reba, my little sister was laying in a hospital holding on to life. If I had just taken one of the calls, I would have known about my little sister.

As I entered the Emergency wing of the hospital and approached the information desk, a silver headed nurse asked if she could help me. "Yes, I am looking for the room of Chantal James who was admitted yesterday." Oh yes, she is in room 554, are you a relative?" "Yes I am. I am her brother." "Sir, I had to ask because only immediate family is allowed in her room at this time." As I entered the elevator headed for the fifth floor, I couldn't help but feel that I had let my family down by not being here. What had happened to my little sister while I was out pleasuring myself?" How selfish could I have been? I just didn't know, I didn't know."

As I got off of the elevator, my heart was beating as if it was going to jump out of my chest. The first person I saw was Aunt Doll who stopped me before entering the room. "What happened to Chantal Aunt Doll?" "We don't know yet baby but what we do know is that she was beaten pretty badly and sexually assaulted on her way home from school. Someone painted the word "PAY BACK" on her legs. The doctor said that she will be OK but will take some time to heal psychologically from the rape. Tears started to roll from my eyes as I slid down the wall to the floor, how could someone do that to Chantal, so young, so innocent? Could something that I had done in the past have caused this? Moms came out to the hall and just stared at me with a disgusted look on her face. "AJ, where were you, we were trying to get you all night. Where were you?" "Moms, please forgive me, I didn't know and I had my phone off because I had been getting so many calls that I didn't want to take. I had agreed to meet an old friend in Indy for a few drinks. I am sorry Moms! Do they have any idea who did this?" No not yet, the only thing that they know is someone observed a Red Mustang with large tires speeding away from the area where Chantal was found. The driver was wearing a hoodie so no one was able to get a clear look at him. There were two others in the car. Sounds like some of the gang bangers but no one knows for sure. They were able to get some faint prints from her purse and some skin where she was able to scratch the attacker. Maybe the cops will be able to get an ID from that.

My mind immediately went to the red Mustang similar to mine, that pulled away just as I was leaving the car wash and Shawn had threatened to get even because of Faye. But Shawn drove a silver Lexus not a Mustang.

I will find who did this to my little sister if it's the last thing that I do, you can bet on that. Pookie had also warned me about someone who may have something against me. I could not live with myself it I caused this to happen to Chantal.

I finally mustered up enough nerve to go in to see Chantal. I was horrified to see what had been done to that pretty little girl, my sister, my special blessing from God. Her face was swollen, scratches were on her arms and neck and IV tubes were running in her arms and nose. I couldn't help but turn away and in an instant started to punch the wall over and over until blood flowed from both hands. Suddenly I felt strong hands grab my shoulder and hugged me tightly. It was my Pops. I couldn't remember the last time that he showed any emotion toward me or told me he loved me but it was better late than never." AJ, it's all right son, it's all right. We will find who did this to our baby." I pulled away slightly and looked in Pops eyes and for the first time, I believed him. There was fire in his eyes that I had never seen before. "Pops, no doubt, we will find the sick sucker who did this or we will die trying."

Just then, a slight noise came from Chantal. She was calling my name in a hushed voice. I quickly rushed to her bed side and leaned over to see if I could make out what she was saying. The only thing I could here was the word "white." Was she trying to tell me that it was a white boy who did this? Before I could ask her to repeat it, her eyes closed and she was back into a deep sleep from the anesthesia. "AJ, could you hear what she was saying", said Aunt Doll." "No, I couldn't make it out. Maybe she will try again when she wakes up." I didn't want the family to know what Chantal had said because if I find out that it was Shawn that had violated my little sister, I will terminate his ass and won't think twice about it.

With all of Pookie's connections to the streets, there should be someone who can give us an idea of what happened to Chantal. Guys who do this type thing eventually want to share it with someone and I hope he does. At this point, nothing matters other than finding out who did this. I was feeling guilty for not being here for Chantal, for not being here when the family needed me.

I left the hospital in a daze. I was determined to spend the time and money tracking down this low life that hurt Chantal. I had rediscovered my Pops but came close to losing my sister. Could Shawn be behind this or could he have hired someone else to commit the crime? After all, he had threatened to get even with me and the words "PAY BACK" written on Chantal's legs seem to indicate that her attacker was looking for revenge but on whom? Chantal was loved by all who knew her in the neighborhood.

After leaving the hospital, I rode around for it seemed like 2 hours looking for the red Mustang before returning to my crib for some much needed rest. I couldn't get the image out of my mind of Chantal laying cut and bruised in that hospital bed. It was a sleepless night and I woke up constantly feeling helpless. Revenge was the order of the day and I would not rest until I had it. Could this have just been a random attack and Chantal was just in the wrong place at the wrong time?

Later that evening, I got a call from Moms asking that I come over to meet with the detectives who thought that they might have a lead. I hurried to Moms apartment in hope that there was enough to burn the son of a mother who did this to Chantal. As I walked into the apartment, Moms introduced me to Detective Hathaway of the Chicago PD. "Detective, this is our son AJ, we wanted him here to hear what evidence you have." "Good to meet you son. We were fortunate that we were able to get some good tissue samples and a print from the crime scene thanks to your daughter's actions. Evidently, in her attempt to fight them off, she was able to get them to grab her purse probably while she was hitting them. She was also able to scratch one of them during the attack. The print is one of a person by the name of Alex Brower. There is no criminal record on this guy but he was involved somehow." Do either of you know of anyone by that name?" Mom and Pops said no and they looked at me.

I nodded no but in the back of my mind I knew that Shawn's friend from the hotel was named Alex. "Detective, what about the

DNA from the skin sample?" "Well son, another fortunate result though it was someone else that had no past criminal record. It was from a guy named Shawn Samuels. We check all of the gang activity and these are not listed a gang members."

When I heard Shawn's name, my heart dropped. I said to myself, "I knew it, I knew it, and I knew it." I was hoping that the detective didn't see me clinching my teeth and fist as Shawn's name was called. "Well folks, we have our detectives out on the street looking for these thugs and we hope to have them real soon." I whispered under my breath, "I hope not if I get to them first." Mama, said, "Thanks detective for all that has been done to fine these animals." "You are welcome Mrs. James; we will make sure that they don't do this to some other person."

I returned to my apartment to decide my next move. It was Shawn who had raped my little sister and he would pay dearly for that. It was Sunday morning and still no word from Ashley. My macho would not let me call her again. There was still a slight drizzle outside and I had no desire to go out other than the fact of not having anything in the frig. As I settled to watch a little TV, Pookie call and wanted me to meet him at Joe's Crab Shack. Maybe he had heard about what happened to Chantal. I didn't think to ask him while on the phone. He sounded rushed so I threw on a pair of jeans, a sweat shirt and my pull over sweater and rushed to meet Pookie not just to hear him ramble on about nothing but because Joe had some of the best Barbeque Ribs on this side of town. I had decided not to mention what I knew about the attack to anyone until I had decided my next move. As I rolled up to the parking lot, Pookie was waving his arms frantically for me to stop. "AJ, are you ready for this. "Ready for what, are you going to tell me who hurt my little sister?" "Your little sister . . . you mean someone hurt Chantal?" "Yes, I thought you knew. When I find out who did this, there is not enough real estate on earth to hide the dude. Man someone followed her from school and beat and raped her something awful." "That's really sick and I will ask around to see if anyone heard or saw anything." I was hoping you would say that Pookie, you are my boy." "AJ, that's the least I can do and if I find the sucker before you do, his ass is grass and I am the lawn mower." "Nah Pookie, if you find him I need to know because I have a score to settle. No one does that to my little princess and live to tell about it. I swear, I will cut his balls off and push them down his throat."

"Now Pookie, what was it you got me down here to tell me?" "This doesn't seem important now AJ, but what I called you down here for is that Ashley is in the Shack with another dude. I didn't want you to freak out over the phone." "No big deal Pookie, it's probably one of the dwebes that she works with." "I don't think so my brother with blinders on, they are too cozy to be just working buddies." As I entered the restaurant, I could see Ashley sitting with her back to me and the guy she was with was draped all over her. As I approached the table where they were sitting, I wondered how she would react once she recognized me. I called out, "Ash, is that you." "Oh, hi AJ, a little surprised to see you here." "That I am sure of Ashley and aren't you going to introduce me to your friend?" "I hadn't planned to but since you asked, Raphael, this is AJ, AJ, this is Raphael and in case you are wondering AJ, he knows all about you." Though I had accused her of being surprised to see me, she really didn't seem surprised at all. In fact she acted as if she didn't give a dam whether I saw her or not. I may have pushed Ash over the line this time. I wanted my cake and eat it too but it seems that Ash had closed the dessert line.

"Why haven't I heard from you Ash, we were going to get something to eat yesterday, what's up?" Spare me the drama AJ, you don't have time for me and I don't have time for your games." "The days are over that I set around and wait for you to get around to me, I am moving on. And by the way, I hope you had a good time with your "FRIEND" in Indy." Ash said it like she knew why I was in Indy. Did she know that I was with Reba and is just playing me?" It was hard for me to be upset after spending the night with Reba, so I put on my mack face and played it off as if it was nothing." Yo Raphael, good meeting you dude, you guys have a nice day and take care of Ash, she is a good woman." I gave Ash a final look and walked toward the exit. If she wanted a hot dog over this T-bone steak, then it's her call. I have to admit that it pissed me off to see her sitting there with that dwebe draped around her. Pookie was waiting outside staying away from what he thought would be fireworks. "What's up man, you OK?" Yea man, I'm cool. She is pissed at me for not taking her to a work function this weekend so she decided to step out on me but I'm cool."

As I returned to my apartment, I could hear the phone ringing as I entered the door. "Hello", "hello AJ, I didn't want us to end that way, so I wanted to call and tell you that I couldn't do this anymore. I was not your priority and it was becoming painfully obvious. I received a call from someone telling me that you were in Indy to meet an old girl friend. Is that true AJ? I just need to know the truth." "Ash, I didn't want to hurt you but my old friend was in Indy for a conference and agreed to meet me for a drink. She is just a friend and we got a little carried away with the celebrating and I was in no condition to drive home so I got a room for the night and I should have told you." "AJ, you see what I mean about priorities, whoever she is, she was your priority and not me. I need someone in my life that I can trust and I can't trust you anymore. It's best that we give each other some space and I wanted to tell you that. Good-bye AJ."

As we hung up the phone, I realized how much of a mess my life was and now it had spilled over into my relationships. Ash had been good to me and I again had blown yet another relationship because of my bush league actions. As much as I cared at one time about Reba, it was Ashley that had stood by me and I had let her down. I was determined to make it up to Ash in some way, I owe her that much even if she never takes me back. I tried flowers, candy and calls to Ash after that and she never responded.

For the next couple of weeks, I drove around looking for Shawn and his posse. They were nowhere to be found. Maybe they had left town trying to wait until the current situation clears. They were probably unaware that they were wanted by the Chicago PD and now me. From that point, it was off to work and back home. I didn't answer the phone nor hang out in the normal places. I just wanted to get my head straight and try and refocus my life. Seeing Reba and how well she has done makes me realize that life is more than good sex and a few dollars in your pocket. From this point on, I will dedicate my time to finding Shawn and Alex.

It was 8:00pm and Pookie had been snooping around for weeks trying to find a lead. I didn't want to let him know that I knew who did this and their asses were mine. I really didn't want to get him involved in what I was going to do to those suckers. Pookie was known to be a blood hound so we got the break that we had been hoping for. While shooting pool at the pool hall on the corner of Hillside and Baker, Pookie overheard a conversation between two white guys who were sitting at the bar and who obviously had over indulged in mixing beer and Alcohol. One guy was tall and well built and the other was short and stocky. The taller more athletically built guy was bragging about something he had done in retaliation for someone who had wronged him. He went on to say how he had hit the guy's sister in retaliation and was laughing hysterically about it. Pookie, got on the phone to call AJ.

"AJ, we may have hit pay dirt. I am at a little sleazy bar on Hillside and Baker. I overheard this conversation that I am sure you will be interested in. These two white guys were talking about hitting some dude's sister in retaliation for something. One dude was named Alex and the other was that dude that you went to school with name Shawn. I have seen you guys talking a time or two." "Pookie, are you sure? Are you sure what you heard?" "AJ, get your ass down here right now before they leave."

Was this the break that I have been looking for? Shawn had violated Chantal and would not live to see tomorrow if I could help it. I had a Saturday night special in my car that just may come in handy. I got dressed and headed to meet Pookie. After arriving at the bar, I walked into the side entry so that anyone sitting at the bar could not see me. I spotted Pookie sitting in a booth directly across from where 4 men and a woman were sitting at the bar. Two of the men were definitely Shawn and Alex. After a few minutes had passed, Alex stood up to leave but Shawn remained. They exchanged farewells and parted ways.

"Pookie, are you absolutely sure what you heard, because if you are, these guys won't leave here alive"??" "Wait AJ, What are you talking about, man you better call the cops. I will tell them what I heard." "Pookie, it would be your word against their word and I don't hold a lot of hope that they will believe you over a white boy. It doesn't matter anyway because the cops already know that these dudes did Chantal and are looking for them too. Here is what I want you to do. I want you to go over to the bar and strike up a conversation with Shawn while I take care of his buddy that just left. Tell him that you over heard his conversation and that you know he was talking about me because my sister was attacked and is in the hospital." "Can you do that Pookie? If he bites on that, then we got the sucker."

While Pookie was preparing to approach Shawn, I hurried to catch Alex. I followed him a ways from the bar where he had parked his car on a dark street next to a vacant lot. As he opened the door, I shouted out, "Yo Alex, what's up my white brother." "Is that you AJ? What are you doing around here man." "Just so happens I am looking for you my perverted friend." "Looking for me for what?" "My little sister wanted me to say hello." It was obvious that he knew now why I was there and was obviously nervous because he dropped his keys. As he bent down to pick them up, I hit him with the butt end of the pistol. As he laid there begging me to not shoot him, he started to talk. "AJ please, don't shoot me, it was Shawn who raped you sister. I had nothing to do with it." "Yea, but you were there and did nothing to stop it." "Yes, I was there but what could I do, you know how Shawn is man." "That's too bad Alex because you are guilty for being his friend and it was your other buddy's skin under my little sister's fingernails." As I loaded a round in the chamber, he held his hand up to cover his face. I screwed on a silencer as to not have the sound detected. "AJ MAN, I'M SORRY, I didn't want him to hurt anyone . . . . please man, I didn't do nothing." "Yes Alex, you are sorry, and I am sorry for what I am about to do . . . . This is for Chantal . . . pop . . . . pop and this one is for being a dumb coward . . . pop . . . pop. It was easier than I thought. I could only think of Chantal and not the lifeless body laying crumpled in the street at my feet. Luckily, the streets were deserted and I was hoping that no one observed what I had just done. I grabbed him by his feet and drug him into some high brush in the adjacent vacant lot and covered him with cardboard and trash. As I reentered the Bar from a side door and waited in the shadows, I could hear clearly the conversation between Pookie and Shawn.

Pookie was sitting to the right of Shawn. Shawn glanced over at Pookie and without hesitation said, "What's up?" "Man, I overheard you and your friend talking about getting revenge for something that someone had done to you. I just happen to know that a guy name AJ was telling people about his sister being raped and beaten. It's not my business but I have never liked that dude and though I feel sorry for his sister, he got what was coming to him. I have been looking forward to getting back at that guy since he clipped me for some money when we were in jail." Shawn was beginning to feel more comfortable with Pookie and started to loosen up and talk. "Yea, man, you have nothing to worry about because your debt has been paid." "That young tender thing was easy picking and now part of my revenge is complete." With a big smile and a wink, Shawn got up to leave, paid his tab and started out the front entrance. I gave AJ the thumbs up and he left through the side door. I felt like cold cocking the son of a mother right there knowing now what he had done to Chantal. Pookie hurried out to find AJ holding a gun to Shawn's head.

"I finally got your ass Shawn. Now tell me what you were bragging about in the bar. "What the hell are you talking about AJ?"

At that point, Pookie rounded the corner to the alley where AJ was holding Shawn. "AJ, I overheard that punk laughing about what he did to Chantal and he admitted it to me at the bar." "Shawn laughing said, "It's my word against yours and who do you thinks the cops will believe?" "Unfortunately for you, you are so right Shawn and that why this has to end right here, right now." I didn't want to tell him that the cops knew that he was a part of the rape of my sister. If the cops got to him first, he may get off too easily and I can't have that. "You are a big man with that gun in your hand AJ, said Shawn." "Well, this is for Chantal and the first shot rang out striking Shawn in the right upper thigh, a second shot hit him in the left lower leg, the third in the shoulder and the 4th in the chest. It was indeed AJ's intention to end it there. As AJ raised the gun for the final time and pointed it at Shawn's head, police sirens pierced the night air. AJ and Pookie, realizing the gravity of the situation, took off toward the other end of the ally. I told Pookie to go it alone because that may be looking for two of us. As Pookie and I arrived back at the crib, I realized that unless Shawn had died, we would get a visit from the police very soon. Pookie was in better shape as far as the cops were concerned because Shawn never knew his name

Several days passed and no cops came to my door. Had Shawn died? Was he in a coma? The phone rang and I was afraid to answer. It rang a second and third time and finally I had to answer. It was Pookie. "AJ, I heard that that guy Shawn was going to survive and that he was not talking to anyone including the cops. What's that about? Why would he protect you after what you did?" "I don't know Pookie, I have to be prepared for anything." At that point, a knock was at the door. As I looked through the peep hole, it was Pops. He had never set foot in my place so what was this about." I opened the door and welcomed him in. "AJ, any luck in finding out who violated Chantal? "Pops, the less you know about this, the better. If they come looking for me, you are still around to protect the family. It wouldn't do to have us both in jail. Last night, I caught up with the guy that abused Chantal and I shot him 4 times. Before I had the chance to finish the job, the cops came and I ran before they saw me. The dude is still alive and why he hadn't rated me out, I don't know. Pops, I wanted him to suffer like Chantal did. I wanted to punish him before ending his life." Well son, I'm glad that you didn't because attempted murder is no comparison to murder. He is still alive and I too have mixed feelings about that. I have a detective friend down at the Court house that I will talk to on your behalf. He will understand that it was because of the abuse to your sister that you did what you did. Thanks son, it won't fix what happened to Chantal, but to know that he has suffered as a result of what he did gives me some comfort. Pops was a man of his word and after sharing what Pookie had overheard between Shawn and Alex plus the evidence to Pops detective friend, I was released and placed on two year probation. Shawn, after confessing to the rape was given 7 years with early release for good behavior. That was still too good for what he did and I will not forget it.

Alex's body was found sometimes later and assumed to be a victim of the surrounding drug wars. There had been many unsolved murders in that area so the cops just added another. I was feeling a lot of grief for taking a life and I was sure that it would catch up to me later. The gun that I used had been deposited in the river and, to that point had not been found.

A few weeks had passed and my life was in a shambles. I had not heard from Ashley or Reba so I decided to finally test my assumption on Portia. "Hello Portia, it's AJ from the car wash, remember?" "Oh yes, AJ . . . . and there was a long pause . . . what's up?" "I thought that maybe we could have a burger or something to get to know each other. I have to admit, I need a friend right about now." "Well AJ, I don't know." "Please Portia, I just need a little female companionship and it's straight on the up and up." Another Pause from Portia before she said, "OK AJ, maybe coffee and a sandwich would work. What about the little coffee shop on King drive near the old Howard Theater?" I will meet you there around 5:00 pm.

I arrived at the coffee shop a little early so that I could get a good seat and observe Portia when she entered. I am still a little unsettled oh how we met. Portia arrived wearing a short leather skirt hugging every curve and inch of her gorgeous body. I stood to greet her and we both slid into the little tight booth area. "Hi AJ, it's good to finally meet you. I thought you had pitched my number the same evening that we met. You must understand why I feel that way after giving a girl the cold shoulder as you did." "Portia, it was just the wrong time and the wrong place. I was going through a lot then and I had no room for anything or anyone at that point. I was a little curious as to why you gave a brother that kind of attention." "What you will find out about me Mr. AJ . . . is that I am not shy when I see something I want.

Portia ordered a decaffeinated coffee and a bagel while I had a fully-loaded cup of high octane coffee because I needed the caffeine. I topped it off with a piece of apple pie. "So Portia, tell me about yourself, why did you give this brother so much play at the car wash a few months back?" "Well AJ, like you needed a friend, I thought you were a nice guy and not hard to look at. What about you?" "Well Portia, I don't know if you read about it in the papers but my baby sister was molested and severely beaten by a guy who was trying to get revenge because I dated his girl." He followed her home from school and beat and molested her. She was just recently released from the hospital. I shot the dude four times but did not kill him though I would have if the cops had not arrived.

I am not a violent person but I see red if someone messes with my family. His name was Shawn." As soon as I said his name, Portia almost choked on her coffee and her beautiful mahogany skin turns pale. "Are you OK Portia?" Yes, I am ok, just drinking a little too fast." "What did this guy Shawn look like AJ?" "He was just a buff white boy who loves black women." Portia acted like she had seen a ghost. All of a sudden, she was ready to leave. "AJ, sorry for having to cut our visit short but I am not feeling well. Maybe we can do this another time." "Ok Portia, I'm sorry that you are not feeling well. Please call me if you want to continue our conversation." Portia left in a hurry. Her reaction really was suspicious. Did she know Shawn? Was it more than coincidental that we met at the car wash just prior to Chantal's rape? Had Shawn put her up to meeting me or trying to set me up? You can bet that this is not over. As long as Shawn is alive, my life will be unsettled.

As Portia left the Café she reflected on what had just happened. "Did I hear what I thought I had heard? Did Shawn really rape that little Girl and try to use me to get even with AJ? I have to know for sure if Shawn did what AJ seems to think he did." Portia dialed Shawn number and it had been disconnected so she tried the hospital and sure enough, he had been being treated for gunshot wounds and had been released in the custody of the Police. "That dirt bag tried to use me to do his dirty work. I hope he rot in hell.

I made my way through traffic to the hospital to see Chantal and to see if she can clearly tell me what happened. When I arrived at her room, she was setting up in the bed staring out of the window. She had lost her innocence and her life was changed forever." "Chantal . . . . Chantal", I called out. Chantal never changed her focus from the window. Tears came to my eyes because I could see the damage, the hurt, the embarrassment that she would have to deal with at such a young age. Killing was too good for Shawn; he had to suffer the way that Chantal has.

I searched around and found that Shawn had been placed at the Metropolitan Correctional Center where I had taken up residency for a short period of time. I still had a few connections inside the walls. The whole while I was in there I stayed close to the wall to protect my back side from the horny piss ants who had not seen a woman for quite a while. When the hard core Alpha males set their sights on me, I was given a pass because of a monster of a man they called Red Brown. Red saw me as his little brother and looked out for me while I served my time. This dude had arms like tree trunks, tattoos from head to toe and a temper that even frighten the guards, and a set of eyes that set back in his head like he had been drinking cough syrup all of his life. Back on the block, that cough syrup screwed up many bad ass dudes who thought they could handle it. When Big Red spoke even EF Hutton listen. The man had a soft side until he was crossed. You would rather walk through hell with Kerosene draws on rather than screw with Red.

I waited a few days for Shawn to settle down in his new digs before letting him know that I had not gone away. Visiting hours were from 3:00 o'clock until 6:00 so on the following Monday, I made it a point to be there to visit Red Brown, a drug dealer and bouncer who was serving time for stabbing a restaurant worker 12 times for spilling water on his suit. Red had been in and out of prison for petty thief many times before. As we all waited in the room with picnic tables scattered all over this large open area, the prisoners were allowed one at a time to enter the area to be greeted by their visitors and take a seat at the table. As Shawn entered the room, I was standing near the entry way and our eyes met.

Shawn immediately moved in my direction and was subdued by the guards. "You will pay for what you did to me and you can bet on that AJ." "And you will pay for what you did to my little sister, you frickin pervert." At that point a shadow came over the room when Red Brown came into the area to meet me. He had overheard part of the conversation. "AJ, WHAT'S COOKING MY LITTLE BROTHER?" "Red that son of a MOTHER standing over there RAPED MY LITTLE SISTER." Red, snapped his head around in the direction of Shawn. "This piece of shit raped little Chantal? Oh, hell no, hell to the no." Red's eyes turned blood shot and sweat started to pour from underneath his toboggan cap like rain on a window Payne. Red, pointed at Shawn and slowly walked away. "Good seeing you AJ . . . . I got it", was all he said as he was escorted by the guards back through the corridor. Shawn, realizing that he now could have an inside problem, slowly moved to a corner of the room and took a seat at a table keeping his eyes on me. As I turned to leave, I wondered who would visit this looser. I waited another 30 minutes and just as I started to leave, in through the center of the room walked none other than Portia.

My intuition was right, she did know him and her reaction at the coffee shop, gave her away. As I watched their interaction, I could see an argument starting. Shawn reached for Portia's arm and she pulled away. I could tell it was a heated exchange. I stood inside of the door so that I could be seen by both. Shawn pointed in my direction and Portia put her hands to her mouth and hurried to the door to leave. With a big smile on my face, I placed my finger to my throat in a cutting motion as he had once done, then pointed my finger in a shooting motion as if to say, I got you now you scum bag. I knew that Red Brown would take care of business. I later got the word that Shawn had been sexually abused over and over by Red's boys and was a broken man. The last I heard of him was that he was living in some half way house across town and surviving the best he could. What a come down from the glory days of big money and hot black women. He is seen around town from time to time but seemed to be a broken man. Chantal, with the help of therapy and much love from my family has made significant progress and was back in school.

I saw Portia once after that and she broke down and cried. She did everything that she could to convince me that even though she knew Shawn, she had nothing to do with his sleazy plan to hurt Chantal. Portia turned out to be one of my best confidents and friends and she had my back no matter what. No I didn't hit it because I didn't feel that way about her but she was one fine specimen of a woman. Ashley had dropped her new play toy and had tried several times to rekindle our relationship. Though I had to spend some time revisiting Faye and her sexual ways and even made a few trips to visit Reba, I knew that Ashley was the one who I could depend on. The thing I most like about Ash is that she like me for me, while the others were just about the sex thing.

I spent a lot of time working and reflecting on my life, my relationship and my family from that point. Taking Ash out for a nice night on the town was really nice. I finally realized that doing special things for her and going places with her showed her how important she was to me and how special our relationship was. I was finally satisfied just being with her. Faye had her new life as a designer and Reba as a big time prosecutor in New York City and after all these years, I was still afraid of the dark.

There was one thing about Chicago summers, if you waited long enough, another one of those electric storms would come through the area. The weather report had said that the storm was 24 hours away but boy did they miss this one. As the clouds rolled in, Lightning illuminated the night as if it was mid day. I glanced at the clock on the stove and it was blinking on an off from the storm. I had laid down to rest for a few minutes which ended up being a couple of hours, I was exhausted and the last couple of month's activities was finally catching up to me.

On this dark and stormy evening as the wind played a tune as it whistled between the buildings, the rain came down in sheets while the larger than normal drops banged against the window pane like gun shots. I stood looking out over the sparsely lit streets of my neighborhood still trying to understand the strange feeling that had dominated my mind since leaving work. I couldn't help but wonder just what was going on in the allies and corroders of the shanty houses bordering the streets at the corner of 15th and Broadway. In fact, just looking at the rain glistening off the concrete and seeing the yellow glow of the lights from the apartments along the street sort of gave the old place a feeling of peace and for that fleeting moment, my own little heaven. I pressed my nose against the window pane and the warmth of my breath caused a dreary fog on the surface. My mind revisited the beat down that Shawn had given me years before, the steamy and exhausting sex episodes with Faye and Reba, the difficult times with Ashley and the friendship with Portia. I thought about the sacrifices that my parents had made for me and the terrible thing that had happen to Chantal. My life had been a series of missed steps and my focus had been on the wrong things. As tears welled in my eyes, a single drop broke away from the rest and headed down my cheek and landed in my hand.

I raised my head and focused on the street below, I could see a small dog running for cover to get out of the drenching downpour while other dogs braved the elements to fine a morsel of food from the garbage cans on the curb, to satisfy their extraordinary hunger. I could identify with them because the hunger pains were beginning to hit me as well. A police car with its siren blasting headed for another forgettable or unforgettable circumstance. Whenever I hear that sound, I breathe a sigh of relief that they are not coming for old AJ, this time. I had spent more than my share of time in the back of those Police cars looking through the chicken wire barrier that separates the pigs from the innocent people like me who was accosted and carried to jail for simply being WWB, (walking while black).

As I glance over the bars that covered the windows, I could not help but wonder what it would be like to, like the TV program *I Dream of Genie,* just wiggle my nose and I would be transferred telepathically to another place and time, away from the dark streets with broken street lights, away from the constant gun fire of both police and gang warfare, away from the rooms with barely enough heat to keep us warm during these hard Chicago winters, away from the absentee dads and cocaine addicted mom, away from the crying of my little sister because she was hungry, away from the roach filled bedrooms and frig with no food. Day dreaming was part of my pass time because it gave me hope and it was all that I had to hold on to.

As I glanced in another direction toward condemned buildings where junkies and prostitute usually handle their entrepreneur activities on the street, I couldn't help but notice the eerie silence on this night. This was indeed unusual for this street where something was always going down whether good or bad. Just as I turned to walk away and back into the boredom of the flat which reminded me of Fred Sanford's junk yard, a quick final look across the street revealed a shadowy figure appeared from the alley with a red and white Chicago Bulls throw back jersey and a rain soaked New York Yankee ball cap pulled down slightly over his face revealing large bulging eyes and a narrow face which was engulfed with long un-kept dread locks. He had both hands in his pocket as if he was on a mission. As I turned back to the window, I strained my eyes to try and focus on him to see if I recognized this lone figure piercing the silent moon lit street below. He came closer and closer giving me a good vantage point of his movement but I still couldn't see his face. The hood and the cap were perfect covers to protect his identity.

Just as quickly as he stepped upon the curb on my side of the street, our eyes met and in a blink of an eye he removed his right hand from his pocket and I heard a POP, POP, POP. The glass where I was standing shattered into pieces and there I stood looking down at a lifeless body laying at my feet . . . . a warm feeling came over me as I viewed the wet, glass covered linoleum floor beneath my feet where the body laid drenched in blood. The fallen figure seemed so quietly familiar stretched out on the barren floor of my apartment. It took me only a moment to realize that the figure lying cold and still on my floor with his eyes seemly locked on mine . . . . was me. Shawn had gotten his revenge.

Snap out of it and let's get back to reality. No my brothers and sisters, this is not intended to be a murder mystery or a fictional novel but instead the reality of a scenes played out in many of our cities across this land of plenty. It's what seems to have become the rule verses the exception for both innocent and none innocent participants in the war for life.

I know, I know . . . . that I have just whet your appetite for a murder and mayhem novel of greater length. You had prepared yourself for the reading with your class of milk and wine, cheese and crackers. Not so fast . . . . I really need your undivided attention on how young men like AJ could reverse the results of that short story. How do we transform his hope to an eventual reality? I wanted to draw your attention to how young men can keep themselves out of situations like this character did. AJ was not able to find his way to the light switch. He was unable to make the ultimate decision to change his destructive direction. At some point in all of our lives we get to the cross roads like AJ did and sometimes we make the wrong decision. All wrong decisions do not take you to a dark place like AJ put himself. The key here is to learn from your mistakes and not repeat them.

My intent here is to show that there may be a dark side to any of us and circumstances like the abuse of young Chantal could be the trigger point as it was for AJ who was not the type of young man that had experienced a life of murder. He made some bad decisions that followed him and eventually led to his death. There are a lot more AJ's out there and I hope this short novel will show how staying close to family, getting a good education and respecting women is are the right tools for the tool kit.

Am I my brother's keeper? . . . . is a question that should be answered by each of us as brothers, men, husbands, fathers and concerned citizens. What intrigues me about that is, unlike other cultures, we black men has gone through so many phases and challenges to our manhood. Luckily many of us have not met the fate that our friend AJ did though still so many have.

From the early days of slavery when we black men were used like animals to breed, many were stripped of their dignity on the auction block, taken away from their families and deposited on plantations miles from their children and wives. Others were beheaded, hanged and castrated, and as a result, men of color have had a difficult time reestablishing our rightful place as heads of our families. We have had to muster up all of the testosterone and courage to move from the victim to the victor. These acts of crime, yes I said crime, left undeniable scars on our image as leaders of our families, our communities and most of all our self esteem.

Any time there is a deep cut in the skin, a resulting scar appears that is a constant reminder of the events that created that cut. Once anything is damaged, it is much more difficult to return its original form. A broken arm, a damaged heart, your car after an accident, and a relationship after a betrayal of trust, all are forever damaged no matter how hard you try to fix them. They may look the same on the surface but underneath, there are scars reminding you of the damage. In addition to these scars are life's little constant reminders that the damage happened in the first place. It's like we are constantly looking over our shoulders because it's hard for us to trust anyone or anything.

These atrocities even sometimes caused our black women to question whether we were capable of leading because of the daze and depression that the scars had caused. If we lose the trust of our mothers, daughters and wives, it's like losing your man hood. It cuts deeply into the male ego and survival mentality. Without hope, we can't survive.

There is always some writing or poem that sums up your subject in a way that really bring the point home about how we live our lives and here is such an article. It called "Mayonnaise Jar & Two Beers." I could not find the author of this piece of work but the credit goes to him or her. It goes like this: A professor stood before his philosophy class and had some items in front of him. When the class began, he wordlessly picked up a very large and empty mayonnaise jar and proceeded to fill it with golf balls. He then asked the class if the jar was full and they agreed that it was. The professor then picked up a box of pebbles and poured them into the open jar. He shook the jar lightly and the pebbles rolled into the open area between the golf balls. Then he asked the students again if the jar was full and they again agreed that it was. The professor next picked up a box of sand and poured it into the jar. Of course the sand filled up everything else. He asked once more if the jar was full and the students responded with a unanimous "yes." The professor then produced 2 beers from under the table and poured the entire contents into the jar effectively filling the empty space between the sand. The students laughed. "Now", said the professor as the laughter subsided, "I want you to recognize that this jar represents your life." The golf balls are the important things—your family, your children, your health, your friends and your favorite passion—and if everything else was lost and only they remained, your life would still be full.

The pebbles are the other things that matter like your job, your house and your car. The sand is everything else—the small stuff. If you had placed the sand in the jar first, he continued, "There would be no room for the pebbles or the golf balls. The same goes for life, if you spend all of your time and energy on the small stuff, you will not have room for the things that are important to you. Pay attention to the things that are critical to your happiness. Spend time with your children. Visit your grandparents, take time for your health and periodically get a medical checkup. Be sure to take your spouse out to a nice dinner. Go out and hit the greens and play another 18 holes. There will always be time to clean the house and fix the disposal so take care of the golf balls first because they are the things that really matter in life. Be sure to set your priorities because the rest is just sand." At that point, one of the students raised her hand and inquired about what the beer represents. The old professor just smiled and said, "I'm glad that you asked. The beer just simply shows you that no matter how full your life may seem, there is always room for a couple of beer with a friend."

These are life lessons that we all can identify with. Let's not let our lives get so full of the day to day living that we forget to live.

That we don't take the time to listen to our children, that we fail to give them the nurturing and attention that they need for their development. Sometimes we are so busy flying from place to place to make ends meet, that we become disconnected with those closest to us. When we break the circuit, the light goes out. Reconnect that same circuit, the light returns. As it is with our lives, the relationships that we develop are our circuits and the broken relationships that we develop are the circuit breakers. As long as there is a complete circuit, we are in the light. As soon as the breaker is tripped, we are immediately thrust into darkness. At this point, we depend completely on our touching a nearby object to study or position.

Education and Christianity is our way to the light switch t and all of our way out of darkness. The Journal of Blacks in Higher Education states that nationally, the black student college graduation rate remains a dismally low 43 percent. But the college completion rate has improved by four percentage points over the past three years (2005-2009). As ever, the black-white gap in college graduation rates remains very large and little to no progress has been achieved in bridging the divide. William J. Edwards, Assistant Professor of Biology at Niagara University, stated that, "Education is the source of all we have and the spring board for all our future joys."

Christianity has played a major role in my life. I was forever in church for choir rehearsals, bible study, prayer meetings, etc. These initiatives were a tremendous help in establishing self esteem, character, confidence and belief in God. Religion has been the back bone for many of us no matter the race or culture. It gives us a true beginning as well as helps us determine what is considered right from wrong. It tends to cause us to take the right fork in the road, do the right thing, have a clear conscious, keep our family together, and adds stability to our daily lives. Now, that's how we see it affecting us. How does it affect you? We face a society that can be cajoling and menacing and religion, Christianity, and fellowship has a calming effect on these worldly conditions.

About The Author . . . . .

Ted Bagley, Vice President of Human Resources at Amgen Pharmaceutical Company in Thousand Oaks California, was born in Birmingham Alabama to Ted and Eddie Mae Bagley both deceased. His brother William Bagley, recently retired, resides in Indianapolis with his wife Larnell and daughter Jennifer.

After graduating from high school, Ted joined Uncle Sam's Army where he served in the Old Guard, a ceremonial unit in Ft. Myer Virginia. After serving for several years in that prestigious unit, he was sent to Vietnam at the height of the conflict. At the end of his military career, Ted continued his education at Ohio State University and later graduated from Franklin Business Law School in Columbus Ohio. After college, he joined the General Electric Company's world renowned executive leadership program. After working his way to the executive ranks, Ted left GE to join the Russell Corporation based in Atlanta Georgia. After several years with Russell, he joined Dell Computer in Nashville Tennessee.

His hobbies are bike riding, reading, writing, skating and minor car repair. He has a wife, Debra, Current Chair for the Ventura County Womens Commission, and 4 children, Marcus, Chantal, Christopher and Jared. His passions are: public speaking, counseling, working with young people and exercising. He currently has another piece of his work in Publication. The book's title is, "***My Personal War Within.***" It's scheduled to be released in April 2011.

Edwards Brothers, Inc.
Thorofare, NJ USA
September 15, 2011